**The warm, sweet kiss sent a shower of tingles raining all the way to the tips of her toes.**

When it was over she brought two fingers to her lips and tried to remember how to breathe. "What was that for?"

Her voice sounded shaky, even to her own ears.

Gabe cast a pointed glance upward.

Michelle tilted her head back and followed his gaze. Directly over them were a few dark waxy leaves interspersed with white berries. "Mistletoe?"

"I want this evening to be memorable."

His hands rested on her arms and the heat from his body urged her closer. The scent of his cologne enveloped her and everything—and everyone— around them disappeared until there was only her…and Gabe.

Gabe, the man with the thirteen-year-old daughter.

**Dear Reader,**

Whenever there's talk about what makes a man "hero" material, lots of characteristics get bandied around. Handsome, strong, smart, kind, etc., are some of the more common ones. But sometimes we forget about the less obvious ones. What about a man who will step up to the plate and do what needs to be done, one who takes responsibility for his actions?

Gabe, the hero in *The Doctor and Mr Right*, is that kind of man. When he was little more than a boy himself, he made the sacrifices necessary to be a good father to his daughter. I don't know about you, but to me there's nothing more sexy—and endearing—than a man who is a good dad to his child. If he happens to be handsome—and single, of course—he's even harder to resist!

I really enjoyed writing this book and I hope you enjoy reading it.

*Cindy Kirk*

# The Doctor and Mr Right

# CINDY KIRK

MILLS & BOON

First published in Great Britain 2013
by Mills & Boon, an imprint of Harlequin (UK) Limited.
Large Print edition 2013
Harlequin (UK) Limited,
Eton House, 18-24 Paradise Road,
Richmond, Surrey TW9 1SR

**LP**

© Cynthia Rutledge 2013

ISBN: 978 0 263 23767 2

Printed and bound in Great Britain
by CPI Antony Rowe, Chippenham, Wiltshire

## CINDY KIRK

has loved to read for as long as she can remember. In first grade she received an award for reading one hundred books. As she grew up, summers were her favorite time of year. Nothing beat going to the library, then coming home and curling up in front of the window air conditioner with a good book. Often the novels she read would spur ideas, and she'd make up her own story (always with a happy ending). When she'd go to bed at night, instead of counting sheep she'd make up more stories in her head. Since selling her first story in 1999, Cindy has been forced to juggle her love of reading with her passion for creating stories of her own...but she doesn't mind. Writing for the Mills & Boon® Cherish™ series is a dream come true. She only hopes you have as much fun reading her books as she has writing them!

Cindy invites you to visit her website, www.cindykirk.com

To my wonderful editor, Patience Bloom.
Ours continues to be a fabulous—
and fun—partnership.

# *Chapter One*

"He did not ask you to do that to him." Lexi Delacourt's voice brimmed with laughter.

"He did." Dr. Michelle Kerns had her fellow book club members in the palm of her hand. It hadn't a thing to do with the novel they were discussing in a local Jackson Hole coffee shop. When someone mentioned having a problem with the hero in the book using a whip on a horse, Michelle happened to mention Larry's request.

Larry was a pharmaceutical sales rep from Idaho who she'd been seeing. Until she'd discovered he had a thing for whips. Or more specifically, being whipped.

"What did you say to him?" Mary Karen Fisher rested her arms on the table, her eyes wide. For having five children, the RN could be a bit naive about the kind of men out there.

"First, I picked my jaw up from the floor." Before continuing, Michelle glanced around to make sure no one at any of the nearby tables was listening. "Next, I told him I wasn't into flailing men with whips. *Then* I made it clear that I wasn't interested in seeing him again."

"You have the worst luck." Lexi sighed. "Have you ever just dated a normal guy?"

Even though Michelle had been in Jackson Hole almost two years this was her first book club meeting. She felt as if she'd finally arrived when she received the invitation to join the group. More than a little nervous, Michelle had done a whole lot of talking.

She'd already shared about her high school boyfriend who turned out to prefer guys, the guy in college who'd forgotten to mention he was married and the one back in Saint Louis who'd stalked her. "There were a few normal ones interspersed among the crazies. My ex-husband, Ed, was a normal guy."

"I didn't know you'd been married before." Mary Karen looked at Lexi. "Did you know?"

Lexi shook her head. The other women at the table appeared equally surprised.

"It was when I was in residency in Saint Louis." Although it had been over three years since her divorce was final, the failure of her marriage still stung. "Didn't even make it two years."

"That had to be tough." Betsy Harcourt covered Michelle's hand with hers and gave it a squeeze. "What happened? If you don't mind my asking, that is."

"Ed was a widower with two middle-school-aged daughters." Michelle kept her tone matter-of-fact. "The girls resented me. Ed sided with them. It was a difficult situation all the way around."

That had been a dark period in her life. When she'd married Ed, Michelle had been convinced it would be forever. Her parents had been married thirty-eight years. No one in her family was divorced. Except her. She hadn't turned her back on the institution. But next time, if there was a next time, she'd look for red flags. Like teenage kids.

"We'll find you a good man." July Wahl glanced at her friends and the other women nodded agreement.

"Thanks for the offer, but I'm plucking myself out of the dating pool for now." Michelle experienced a sense of relief just saying the words. "The only one in my life will be Sasha."

Mary Karen pulled her brows together. "Sasha?"

"It's her dog." Lexi spoke in a tone loud enough for all of them to hear.

"Everyone here knows how much I love my Puffy." A doubtful look filled Betsy's eyes. "But would you really choose to spend time with Sasha over someone like…that?"

The newlywed pointed out the front window of Hill of Beans to a tall man with broad shoulders and lean hips loading supplies into the back of a red pickup. Thick dark hair brushed the denim collar and faded jeans hugged long muscular legs.

Even though Michelle wasn't interested, if she *were* interested, she liked that he was tall. Call her shallow, but she rather enjoyed looking up to a man. And being five-nine, unless she wore flats, there weren't too many men around like that.

"He's one fine specimen," Michelle acknowledged. "At least from the backside."

The women watched for a few more seconds, but the guy never turned in their direction.

"Who is he?" Mary Karen asked. "Anyone know?"

"Doesn't matter." Michelle sipped her latte and resisted the urge to steal another quick glance out the window. "Remember, I have Sasha."

"The dog can keep you company for now." Betsy's dusty-blue eyes held a gleam. "Until we find a man for you."

"Which might not be that easy." Lexi's lips turned up in a little smile. "I mean, Michelle is one picky lady. Heterosexual, single, nonstalker and no fetishes. What does she think we are… miracle workers?"

Michelle pulled into her driveway in the Spring Gulch subdivision just outside of Jackson and chuckled, remembering the conversation in the coffee shop. Most of her friends were happily married and determined to aid in her search for Mr. Right.

But she'd been serious when she'd told them she wanted to step off the dating-go-round. Going out with a new guy was not only a huge time suck but an emotional roller coaster, as well. She'd really liked Larry. He was smart, funny and insanely handsome. Although she knew some women might embrace the whips-and-chains thing, she wasn't one of them.

So here she was, after two months, back to square one. She only wished Larry had made his proclivities known on the first few dates. The mistake she'd made was trying to take things slow. If she'd considered sleeping with him early on, this would have come out and they could have gone their separate ways sooner.

Perhaps with the next guy, she should consider tossing aside her old-fashioned morals and jump in the sack right away. Of course, she reminded herself, that was a moot point because she didn't have any plans to date. At least not anytime soon. Perhaps she'd even take the rest of the year off.

Yes, that would be best. Focus on continuing to grow her ob-gyn practice. Spend more time with Sasha. Perhaps even work on making the town house she'd bought late last year feel more like a home.

Michelle eased the car into the garage. Just before the door lowered, she saw a red vehicle pull into the adjacent driveway. She barely got a glimpse of it before her overhead door shut. It seemed the new owners had finally arrived.

The rumor around the neighborhood was a young couple from out of state had purchased the unit next to her. Michelle only hoped they were quiet. She put in long hours at her medical practice. With only two doctors and a nurse-mid-wife, she got called out often, at all hours of the day and night. When she was home she needed her sleep.

Perhaps she'd have to find a way to mention that to the new owners. Just so they understood—

Michelle shut the thought off before it could fully form. Egad, what was she? Eighty? Before long she'd be complaining about the children run-ning through her flower beds. If she had flower beds. And if there were any children in the up-scale neighborhood of young professionals to run through them.

After heading inside and changing into a pair of shorts and a hot-pink T-shirt, Michelle clamped the leash onto the collar of her golden retriever and took the dog for a run.

By the time they returned, it was almost dinnertime and her neighbor stood outside washing his truck. As she and Sasha drew close, she realized with a start that he was the man from the coffee shop. Only this time she could see that his face was as delectable as his backside.

Tall. Dark. Handsome. Something told her he had a petite blonde wife who doted on her husband's every word. Those kind always did.

Still, Michelle slowed her steps as they reached the driveway. She remembered well the kindness of the neighbors when she'd first moved in and it was time to pay that forward.

"Hi." She stopped a few feet from him and extended her hand. "I'm Michelle Kerns. I live next door. Welcome to the neighborhood."

He looked down for a heartbeat, took off the soapy mitt he'd been using before taking her hand in his. "Gabe Davis. Pleased to meet you."

Electricity shot up her arm. She jerked her hand back in what she hoped was a nonchalant manner.

Her new neighbor had charisma with a capital *C* and the looks to go with it. His eyes were an amber color, his hair a rich coffee-brown. Other than a slight bump on his nose, his features were classically handsome.

Michelle ran her hand across the shiny red fender of his truck, the water rippling beneath her fingers. "What brought you all the way from Pennsylvania?"

He stepped close and the spicy scent of his cologne teased her nostrils. But his gaze remained riveted to her hand, caressing the sleek paint. He cleared his throat. "How did you know we were from there?"

"Your license plate was my first clue." Michelle pulled back her hand. His eyes had turned dark and intense. She could read the signs. He didn't appreciate her touching his truck but was too polite to say so.

"Of course." He lifted his gaze and raked a

hand through his hair and blew out a breath. "It's been a long day."

Then he smiled.

Michelle felt something stir inside her at the slightly crooked grin. Mrs. Davis was a lucky woman.

She glanced toward the house. "Is your wife inside?"

His brows pulled together in puzzlement. "I'm not married."

"For some reason a rumor was going around the neighborhood that a couple was moving in." Michelle stumbled over the words.

"Nope. Just me and Finley."

"Girlfriend?"

"Daughter." The smile returned to his lips. "She's inside unpacking. At least that's what she's supposed to be doing. At thirteen, they're easily distracted."

Michelle heard affection in his tone. And fatherly pride.

*Thirteen.* Chrissy, Ed's oldest daughter, had

been thirteen when they married. A knot formed in her stomach.

"Those are…interesting years," she managed to mutter when she saw he was waiting for a response.

"Tell me about it." He chuckled. "You have kids?"

"No," she said. "No husband. No children. Just Sasha."

Her gaze dropped to the dog who sat at her feet, tail thumping.

Gabe crouched down and held out a hand to the retriever. "Hey, girl."

Sasha sniffed his fingers and her tail picked up speed.

"Nice golden." The man scratched behind the dog's ears. "Finley and I used to have one."

"Used to?"

"Buttercup passed away." At her questioning look, Gabe continued. "She died of cancer last year."

"I'm sorry." Michelle couldn't imagine losing

Sasha. "That must have been hard on both of you."

Gabe nodded, then shifted his gaze back to the dog. "Tell me about Sasha."

"She's a purebred," Michelle said as proudly as if she was introducing him to her child. "She's three."

In fact, she'd picked up Sasha the day her divorce was final. The golden bundle of love at her feet had gotten her through the toughest period in her life. Now she couldn't imagine her world without Sasha in it.

His hands moved along the dog's ribs. A frown furrowed his brow. "Has she always been this thin?"

Michelle's smile faded. "What do you mean?"

"I can feel her ribs."

"Dogs aren't meant to be fat," she murmured even as a chill traveled up her spine. She'd always had to watch Sasha's weight. Being too thin had never been an issue.

"You should have a vet take a look at her."

"You think she could be sick?" She pushed the words past her lips. "Like your dog?"

"All I know is Buttercup started losing weight and we didn't notice it at first. When we did, it was summer and we thought it was no big deal, just her eating less because of the heat." He paused, as if considering how much to say. "Later—too late—we learned golden retrievers are prone to lymphoma. Early diagnosis is critical for survival."

Fear, heart-stopping fear, sluiced through Michelle's veins quickly followed by a healthy dose of self-directed anger. She was a doctor. She should have noticed Sasha's weight loss, not needed a stranger to point it out to her.

"I'll definitely have her checked. I certainly don't want anything to happen to her." Unexpected tears filled Michelle's eyes, but she hurriedly blinked them back before he could notice. "Thank you for caring enough to speak up."

Before she could take a step, she felt his hand lightly touch her arm. She looked up into warm amber eyes. "Just remember, if it *is* something serious, you'll have caught it early."

Michelle considered herself to be a strong, independent woman, but times like this made her wish she had a special someone in her life. A man to wrap his strong arms around her and tell her everything was going to be all right.

After her experience with Larry, she'd begun to believe good men only existed in the movies or in the pages of a book.

The spicy scent of Gabe's cologne grew stronger and Michelle realized that while lost in her thoughts, she'd taken a step closer. Even though a respectable distance still separated her and Gabe, it wouldn't take much to bridge that gap.

She met his gaze. Almost immediately their eye contact turned into something more, a tangible connection between the two of them. A curious longing surged through her veins like an awakened river.

Michelle experienced an overwhelming urge to wrap her arms around his neck and pull him close, to feel the hard muscular planes of his body against her soft curves. To press her lips against his neck and—

"Dad," a young female voice called out. "Grandma's on the phone."

Gabe's hand dropped to his side. He turned toward the house, where his daughter stood on the porch, cell phone in hand. "Tell her I'll call her back."

Michelle took a step back, her heart pounding in her chest. Thankfully the crazy spell tethering her to him had been broken. She tugged on the leash and Sasha stood. "Thanks again for the advice."

"It was nice meeting you," Gabe called to her retreating back.

"You, too," Michelle said without turning around.

Tomorrow, when she saw her friends in church, she was going to tell them they could scratch the guy with the truck off their potential suitor list.

No matter how charming, sexy or caring her

new neighbor was, she now knew he had a teenage daughter. Which meant Gabe Davis was one man she wouldn't have, even served up on a silver platter.

## Chapter Two

Thirteen-year-old Finley stopped at the foot of the concrete steps leading into the small white church and lifted her chin. "I'm not going in."

Gabe expelled a breath and kept a tight hold on his temper. Before they left the house, he and Finley had agreed how the morning would progress. Apparently she'd changed her mind. From all the reading he'd done about adolescents, this behavior was typical for a girl Finley's age.

Unfortunately he only had minutes to remind

his daughter of their agreement before the service began.

"It's not easy for me to walk in there." Gabe kept his tone conversational and matter-of-fact. He'd learned to keep things calm around Finley. "But we have to start somewhere."

"I'm dressed all wrong." She glanced down at her yellow sleeveless dress. When she lifted her gaze he saw the worry in her eyes. "All the girls I've seen have on skirts and tops."

Gabe knew better than to dismiss her concerns or try to placate her. At her age emotions were too volatile. "Perhaps you'll start a fashion trend. After all, you're a big-city girl."

Okay, so perhaps Philadelphia wasn't fashion central, but surely in the minds of middle-school-aged girls, her being from the East Coast counted for something.

Finley's brows drew together and he could almost see her processing his words. Personally he thought she looked lovely. If he didn't think a dad's comment would make the situation worse, he'd tell her so. Finley's hair was the color of rich Colombian coffee. Her blue eyes and fine features were from her mother. In several years she'd be a real heartbreaker.

Gabe pushed the thought from his head. He preferred to ignore the fact the little girl who'd once invited him to tea parties was now old enough to wear lip gloss.

"We need to hurry. I'm not walking in late."

Her words pulled him from his reverie.

She practically sprinted up the steps. Gabe followed behind her, relief filling him.

Although he and Finley had attended church regularly since she'd been a baby, this was a different ball game. New town. New church. And in the fall, a new school. They'd waited to move until early summer so Finley wouldn't have to start at the end of the year.

Now he wondered if that had been a mistake. Finley was already complaining of being lonely. His only hope was that she'd make a friend or two today at youth group. This morning she'd made it clear that she was only staying for the church service, but he still held out hope that he could change her mind.

To make this relocation successful, it was important they both reach out to the community. Gabe had already marked his calendar to attend the next Jackson After-Hours meeting, a chamber of commerce function for young professionals. But attending church was a first step in reaching out.

He realized that wasn't exactly true. He'd met several guys at the Y yesterday. When they'd mentioned they attended this church, he'd decided he and Finley would check it out.

Not knowing how casual the service was, he'd forgone jeans for a pair of navy pants and a button-down shirt. As he walked into the church, it appeared he'd guessed correctly, although he did see some guys in denim and a few older men in suits.

The church appeared to attract a lot of young families. His heart twisted. He wished his daughter could have had the experience of having both a father and a mother. But Shannon had relinquished all parental rights when Finley was still an infant and had shown no interest in her since.

*Her loss,* he told himself for the millionth time.

He started to steer them toward a pew in the back until he saw all the parents with babies. Obviously the last few rows were reserved for those with small children.

Gabe continued down the aisle. He wasn't sure what to feel when he saw a tall woman with long wavy blond hair a couple of pews ahead. He recognized her immediately. His neighbor. Michelle.

She was slender with long legs and curves in all the right places and big blue eyes. She appeared to be alone and he thought for a second about sitting beside her. But he wasn't sure that was wise after what had happened in the driveway yesterday.

He'd almost kissed her. He'd *wanted* to kiss her. Yet, making such a move on a new neighbor could have disastrous consequences. After all, they'd just met. And while she'd said she wasn't married, she hadn't said anything about not having a boyfriend. A woman as pretty as she had to have some guy in the wings.

"Gabe," a deep voice sounded behind him.

He spun on his heel to find one of the men he'd met yesterday playing basketball. There was a toddler in his arms. A pretty dark-haired woman and a girl about Finley's age flanked him.

"Nick." Gabe frantically searched for the last name. "Delacourt."

"You nailed it." Nick flashed a smile. "This is my wife, Lexi, and our daughters, Grace and Addie."

They stepped aside to let the other members of the congregation pass while completing the introductions. After Finley's comments outside, Gabe couldn't help but notice that Addie, Nick's oldest daughter, wore a denim skirt and red top.

He pretended not to see the pointed look Finley shot him.

"Most kids our age sit together during the service." Addie focused on Finley and gestured toward a row of young teens seated just ahead of the babies and young families. "You're welcome to join us. If you want, that is."

Finley glanced at Gabe. "Is it okay?"

Gabe quickly assessed the situation. Normally he was very particular about letting his daughter be unsupervised with kids he didn't know. But the church was small and she'd be in plain sight. "Fine with me."

"Afterward we all go to youth group," Addie added. "While our parents eat breakfast."

Gabe could almost see the refusal forming on his daughter's lips when Addie continued in a low tone, "Your dress is really cool. All the girls are going to be jealous."

"You can pick me up after youth group," Finley announced.

Gabe cocked his head and met her gaze. Even though this was exactly what he wanted, in their household, it was understood his daughter didn't call the shots.

"If it's okay with you, that is," Finley quickly added.

He nodded. "Sounds like a workable plan."

Finley squeezed his arm, then hurried off talking in low excited tones with her new friend.

Gabe refocused on Nick's wife. "It was nice to meet you, Mrs. Delacourt."

"Please, call me Lexi." She glanced over his shoulder, then gestured with one hand. "Why don't we sit together? Looks like there's plenty of room."

When Gabe turned to see where Nick's wife pointed, it was the open area next to his neighbor. He hid a smile. Even in church it appeared he couldn't escape temptation.

He followed the couple to the pew. Nick motioned for his wife to go in first, but Lexi shook her head. "Let Gabe."

Her husband looked perplexed. "I thought you'd want to sit by Michelle."

"Oh, we can chat later." Lexi lifted a hand in

a dismissive wave. "It's best I sit by the aisle in case Grace gets fussy."

Gabe had been the focus of too many match-making efforts over the years not to recognize one. Which meant Michelle didn't have a boyfriend. Although for the next six months his priority was settling into his new job and helping Finley acclimate to her new surroundings, he might make time for a date or two.

Acting as if it didn't matter where he sat, Gabe slipped into the polished bench next to Michelle.

She turned from the older couple on her left. "Oh." Her eyes widened. "Hello."

It wasn't quite the enthusiastic greeting he'd expected.

"Good morning," he said politely before shifting his attention to his basketball buddy. But Nick was talking with his wife in a low tone.

"I didn't know you went to church here," he heard Michelle say as the organ began to play.

"This is my first time." Gabe reached for the hymnal at the same time as she did and their hands brushed. He felt an unexpected flash of heat.

If Michelle experienced the same sensation, she gave no indication. When they rose for the opening song, he ended up sharing the hymnal with her. He didn't mind. But he caught her glancing around as if looking for an extra book.

His own singing voice was passable, but Michelle's was, well, simply awful. He couldn't decide if she was tone deaf or couldn't read music. She appeared oblivious to how bad she was, singing loudly and with much enthusiasm.

Gabe cringed as she belted out the last note of the song in a higher pitch than everyone around her.

She closed the hymnal, smiled and sighed. "I love to sing."

"I can see that," he said diplomatically. In an attempt to ignore the enticing scent of her floral perfume, he fixed his gaze on the pastor.

The sermon was a variation of one he'd heard a thousand times but could never hear enough.

The message revolved around good arising out of the trials experienced in life. It was his and Finley's story. An eighteen-year-old kid propelled into being a parent when he was still a boy. Giving up a football scholarship and college to be a father. Shannon walking out of their lives when Finley was only two months old. The road certainly hadn't been easy, but his life was so much richer for having Finley in it.

After making it through a Scripture reading by a woman with a lisp and sharing the hymnal with Michelle for several more off-key renderings, Gabe's ears rang.

After the benediction, Nick turned to him. "While the kids are in Sunday school and youth group, a bunch of us go for breakfast at The Coffee Pot. Care to join us?"

Gabe understood the importance of the invitation. He knew that if he shied away, he might not be invited to join them again. Or if he was, another invitation might be a long time coming.

He glanced at Finley who was laughing with

Addie. He didn't need to ask if she'd changed her mind about staying for youth group. The smile on her face told him the answer.

"Sure. Thanks for asking." Even though Gabe hadn't had a lot of time to explore the town, Jackson wasn't that big of a community. If he knew the approximate location of the destination, he should be able to find it easily. "Where's the café located?"

"It's downtown." Lexi leaned around her husband and flashed Gabe a smile. "Not far, but parking can be a problem. Why don't you leave your vehicle here and ride with Michelle?"

"Michelle?"

"Didn't Nick tell you? She's coming to breakfast, too."

Michelle saw the startled look in Gabe's eyes when he turned. And the Cheshire-cat smile on Lexi's lips.

"What's going on?" When the service ended, Mr. Calhoun, the older gentleman to Michelle's left had started telling her a story and Michelle had missed Gabe and Nick's conversation.

"Gabe is coming to breakfast with us this morning," Lexi said in a pleased tone. "I told him he could ride with you, because parking can be an issue and you know where it is. You don't mind, do you?"

The café was less than a mile away, easy to find with simple instructions. And parking? While Gabe might not be able to park in front of the restaurant, he'd for sure find a space within a block of the building. Lexi knew that as well as she did. The gleam in her eyes suddenly made sense. Her friend was playing matchmaker.

Yet Michelle could hardly accuse Lexi of that in front of everyone. And she didn't want to make Gabe feel unwanted. It wasn't that long ago that she'd been new in town.

"You're welcome to ride with me." Michelle kept her tone light. Just because she didn't want to date the guy didn't mean she couldn't be sociable. "If you want to, that is."

Gabe smiled and her heart fluttered.

During the drive to the café, Gabe asked a lot of questions about her, then listened as if he was really interested in her answers.

Michelle shared how she'd wanted to be a doctor for as long as she could remember, touched on the rigors of med school and residency. Even though she mentioned she'd once been briefly married, she didn't share any specifics about that breakup and nothing about her recent dating challenges.

By the time they entered the café, she realized he knew a whole lot about her and she knew very little about him. Of course, she already knew the most important thing…he had a teenage daughter.

After he opened the door for her, Michelle paused in the doorway. "What made you decide to move to Jackson Hole?"

But she never got an answer. Several other couples came up just then, the men recognizing and greeting Gabe, joking about some basketball game. They introduced him to their wives. By the time they reached the table and sat down, the question was forgotten.

Michelle took a seat at one end of the table. Gabe sat down across from her. Ryan Harcourt, an attorney in town, pulled out the chair next to her, his new bride, Betsy, on the other side of him. Betsy was the best friend of Adrianna Lee, the nurse-midwife in Michelle's office. Ryan and Betsy were eagerly anticipating the birth of their first child in the fall.

"How's the house coming?" Michelle asked Ryan. The young couple were in the process of renovating a bungalow Betsy had inherited from her great-aunt.

"It's starting to feel like home." Ryan glanced at his wife and she nodded. "Of course anywhere with Betsy feels like home."

"You always say the sweetest things." Betsy cupped his face with her hand and kissed him gently on the lips.

Out of the corner of her eye, Michelle caught Gabe staring. Before he turned away she saw something that looked almost like envy in his eyes. Apparently whatever had happened between him and his daughter's mother hadn't left him bitter.

Michelle didn't have time to dwell on the matter because the waitress appeared. The older woman with wiry gray hair and garish orange lipstick moved quickly, knowing most at the table had to be back to the church in an hour to pick up their children from Sunday school.

When it came time for Michelle to order, she didn't hesitate. "I'll have the farmer's breakfast."

By the time she finished giving the waitress the specifics Gabe's mouth was hanging open.

"Can you really eat all that yourself?" he asked with something akin to awe in his voice.

"Breakfast is my favorite meal of the day." Michelle shrugged, telling herself she didn't care what he thought. "I follow that old adage about eating like a king for breakfast, a prince for lunch and a beggar for dinner."

"Well, you certainly look healthy."

The admiration in his tone made her glad she'd taken a little extra time getting ready this morning. Her cobalt-blue sleeveless dress with a beaded belt at the waist not only flattered her figure but the color also made her eyes look extra blue.

"I'll consider that a compliment," she said with a wry smile.

For a second she thought Gabe was going to say more, but then Nick asked him a question. He shifted his attention and she never got it back.

"Come with me to the restroom." Lexi leaned over and whispered, then pushed back her chair and stood.

Michelle followed her around several tables to the small restroom at the back. "I'll wait out here."

"No." Lexi grabbed her arm. "Come in with me."

"It's just a one-seater, Lex—"

"I'm just going to touch up my makeup." Lexi opened the door and shoved her in first, then followed behind. "You can talk to me."

Her friend was up to something. And Michelle had a feeling she knew just what it was. The first words out of Lexi's mouth confirmed her suspicions.

"What do you think of him?" Lexi spoke in a confidential whisper even though they were the only ones in the small room.

"Is that what this is about?" Michelle rolled her eyes and leaned against the wall. "Are you trying to hook me up with Gabe Davis?"

"You have to admit he's a hunk." Lexi's amber eyes sparkled.

"He's good-looking enough, I guess," Michelle reluctantly agreed, hoping the admission didn't come back to haunt her. "But there's no chemistry."

Michelle pushed from her mind the sizzling shock she'd received less than an hour before when her hand had brushed against his across the hymnal. And all those times during the service when she had only to inhale the spicy scent of his cologne for her heart to pick up speed. Of course, glancing back at Gabe's daughter—his *teenage* daughter—was all it took for her heart to return to normal rhythm.

"Oh." Lexi's hopeful expression fell. "No chemistry at all?"

"'Fraid not." Thank God she wasn't Pinocchio or her nose would be a foot long by now.

"His loss." Lexi's face brightened. "I'll find someone else for you."

"Don't bother." Michelle pulled a tube of gloss from her bag and applied some to her lips. "Remember, I've sworn off men."

Lexi fluffed her dark hair with the tips of her fingers, then smiled. "Honey, that's just until we find you the right one."

# *Chapter Three*

Out of the corner of his eye Gabe saw Michelle enter the bar and grill on the edge of downtown Jackson. It seemed in every town there was always one person he was destined to run into again and again. In Jackson Hole, he was lucky enough for that person to be a pretty female doctor.

Gabe grabbed a handful of mixed nuts from the bar and watched Michelle glide across the room. She exuded confidence. It was as much a part of her as her bright smile.

"Gabe."

He turned toward the sound of his name and saw Nick Delacourt at the far end of the curved bar. Dressed in a dark suit, the family law attorney looked as if he'd come straight from court. Gabe lifted a hand in greeting.

Nick started toward him but didn't get far before someone stopped him. In the past fifteen minutes the microbrewery hosting the Jackson After-Hours event had exploded with people. Gabe was glad he'd taken off work a little early. It had given him time to shower and change into a pair of khakis and a green polo with the Stone Craft logo.

Although Gabe had been brought on as a project manager, Joel had made it clear if their business and work styles meshed, he'd have the chance to buy into the company. That meant, what was good for Stone Craft Builders was good for him.

Tonight was Gabe's opportunity to get to know the movers and shakers of Jackson Hole. And for them to get to know him.

Building a client base was all about relation-ships. That's why breakfast on Sunday had been important. But it wasn't only business. Gabe gen-uinely liked the couples who'd been at the table.

"I have a question for you." Tripp Randall, the administrator for the Jackson Hole hospital, re-turned to the bar.

Like Nick, Tripp wore a suit. But the admin-istrator had already loosened his tie and unfas-tened a couple of buttons. Since Gabe had last seen him, he'd also ditched his suit jacket.

With disheveled blond hair and scruff on his chin, Tripp looked as if he should be playing a guitar in a coffeehouse rather than running the area's largest hospital.

Gabe took a sip of beer. "Ask away."

"Have you overseen the construction of many stables?"

It wasn't a question Gabe had anticipated, but he quickly rallied. "Not really, but the great thing about Stone Craft is we can be counted on to do excellent work on any project we take on."

"The company does have a good reputation." Tripp finished off his beer and glanced around the crowded room. "Where's Joel? I thought he'd be here."

"Chloe had a dance recital." Even though normally Gabe wouldn't share such personal information, everyone knew Joel's family was his priority. The desire to spend more time with them had been behind his bringing Gabe on board. Especially because Joel's wife, Kate, had recently given birth to a baby boy.

Family was Gabe's priority, too. That's why working with Joel had been such a good fit.

"Can I get you another draw?" The bartender slid a napkin in front of Gabe.

Gabe shook his head. He'd make the now half-filled glass in front of him last all evening. Since becoming a father he'd lived a disciplined life, knowing the importance of setting a good example for his daughter. He returned his attention to Tripp. "I didn't realize you had horses."

"My dad owns a cutting horse and cattle operation. I know he had trouble with response times from a previous contractor he used." Tripp accepted another beer from the bartender. "If you're interested in bidding, I can put you in touch with his foreman who can give you the specs."

"I'll speak with Joel tomorrow to see what projects we have lined up. But if we can make it work, we'd definitely be interested." Gabe kept any eagerness from his voice. After all, appearing desperate was never good. "What size of stable are you looking—"

"Michi," Tripp called out. "Over here. There's someone I want you to meet."

*Mee-shee,* Gabe thought, *what kind of name is that*?

He turned his head and there she was…again.

Gabe met her gaze and unsuccessfully fought to keep a smile from his lips. "Michi?"

"It's a nickname." Michelle shifted her gaze to the hospital administrator who'd just looped an arm around her shoulders in a familiar manner.

"One you don't have permission to use, Tripp Randall."

The words might have been light, but the look in her eyes said she was serious.

"I didn't know permission was required," Tripp replied with an easy smile. "Adrianna calls you that all the time."

*Adrianna.* Gabe thought back to yesterday's conversation with Michelle. *Adrianna was the nurse-midwife in Michelle's practice.*

"She's my friend," Michelle responded.

Tripp brought a hand to his chest in a movement more suitable for the stage. "And I'm not?"

Michelle glanced upward as if looking to the heavens for assistance. But her gaze quickly returned to the administrator as if realizing there were only heating and cooling ducts in the microbrewery's ceiling. "Of course we're friends. But no, you can't call me Michi. I have an image to uphold in this community."

"You're thinking what?" A teasing glint lit

Tripp's blue eyes. "Women won't want their baby delivered by someone called Michi?"

"Something like that." Michelle's lips quirked upward. "Of course a hospital administrator named Tripp doesn't exactly inspire confidence."

"No respect." Tripp turned to Gabe and jerked a thumb in Michelle's direction. "See what I have to put up with?"

"Well, I'm here to mingle and I'm not getting much of that done talking to you guys," Michelle said before Gabe could respond. She attempted to extricate herself from Tripp's hold, but his arm remained around her shoulder.

"Not so fast." Tripp chuckled. "I have to introduce you to Gabe."

"I already—"

"We already—" Gabe stopped as his words overran hers.

Tripp's gaze lingered on Michelle before returning to Gabe.

"Michelle and I are neighbors," Gabe informed Tripp.

"We also chatted at The Coffee Pot," Michelle added. "Yesterday. After church."

"I'm impressed." Tripp cast a sideways glance at Gabe. "I've been trying to wrangle an invitation for months."

Gabe couldn't tell if the man was being serious or not.

"It's a select group with very rigid requirements." A smile tugged at the corners of Michelle's lips. "Church first. Then the breakfast invitation."

"Harcourt doesn't always go to church," Tripp grumbled. "Yet he's invited."

Gabe figured Tripp must be referring to Ryan Harcourt, of Ryan-and-Betsy, the couple who'd sat next to Michelle.

"Ryan," Michelle said pointedly, "is funny and entertaining."

"That's it." Tripp picked his arm up off her shoulder in a slow, deliberate gesture. "I refuse to take more abuse. I'm going to find someone who appreciates all my fine qualities."

The administrator sauntered off, leaving Gabe alone with Michi, er, Michelle.

He smiled politely. "I didn't realize you came to these events."

"I guess we're even." She took a glass of champagne from a passing waiter. "I had no idea you'd be here."

"We should have ridden together." Even though it wasn't much of a drive for either of them, it would have been nice to have someone to visit with on the way. Not only that, it'd have spared him walking into the event alone.

Michelle simply smiled and glanced around the room.

He had to admit she looked hot tonight in her black dress and heels. Her hair hung halfway down her back in wavy blond curls that shimmered in the dim light. For someone so lean, she was surprisingly voluptuous.

Gabe jerked his gaze from her cleavage. "I've met lots of people tonight. This seems like a prime networking opportunity."

"That's why I'm here." Her gaze continued to scan the crowd.

"You're a doctor." He didn't bother to hide his confusion. "Why would you need to network?"

"My practice is a small one." She refocused on him. "Just me, another doctor and a nurse-midwife. We're competing for patients against one of the largest ob-gyn groups in Jackson Hole. In fact Travis Fisher, one of the guys at breakfast on Sunday, is a partner in that clinic. He's also an excellent doctor."

Gabe took a sip of his now-lukewarm beer. "When you came to Jackson Hole, why didn't you join them?"

"I wanted more autonomy." Michelle lifted one shoulder in a slight shrug. "We deliver very personalized care to our patients and take great pride in that fact."

Michelle smoothed back her hair with one hand, drawing his attention to the creamy expanse of skin of her neck and chest.

His body tightened and Gabe drew air slowly

into his lungs. The intense reaction reminded him how long he'd gone without a woman in his bed.

It had been almost a year. Finley had been in Florida spending a couple of weeks with his parents. He'd been putting in extra hours working construction over the holiday break. One of the accountants in the office was divorced. Neither of them had been interested in anything more than a momentary interlude. It had been satisfying. Pleasant.

But the need coursing through his veins now was a stark carnal hunger. Totally inappropriate for the situation. If there wasn't a Commandment against lusting after your neighbor, there should be.

Gabe pulled his attention from her breasts and asked the question that had been lingering in his head since yesterday. "Why did you and your husband split up?"

Michelle's eyes widened even as her lips tightened.

"You must have loved the guy to have married

him," Gabe persisted. "What went wrong? Do you still see him?"

"Do you ever see your ex?" she shot back.

"Shannon and I were never married." He still felt embarrassed by the admission. In his family it was understood that love came before marriage and marriage came before babies. But Shannon had refused to marry him.

"That doesn't matter. You made a baby together. That makes her your ex."

"Shannon has a new family now." Gabe did his best to keep the bitterness from his voice. He'd never understood—*would* never understand—how Shannon could walk away from her daughter and pretend she never existed. "She's not interested in seeing either one of us."

"Not even her daughter?"

Gabe realized he should have known the conversation would go down this road. But it was a path he had no intention of traveling. The less said about his daughter's lack of relationship with her mom, the better. "I prefer not to discuss Finley or her mother with you."

"Well, I prefer not to discuss Ed and where our relationship went wrong with you." Michelle took a sip of her champagne and cast a wider net around the room with her gaze. He knew she'd found an out when her face lit up. She waved to a strikingly beautiful woman with long chestnut hair standing in the doorway.

"Adrianna came after all," Michelle said with a relieved smile. "I need to introduce her around. If you'll excuse me…"

Michelle strode off without a backward glance.

Gabe lifted his glass of beer to his lips and realized he should have asked her about Sasha instead of her ex-husband. Still, he *was* here to network, not to spend the entire evening talking to the beautiful and sexy woman who lived next door.

But for the rest of the evening Gabe kept one eye on her. Just in case she needed any help of the…neighborly sort.

* * *

For the rest of the week, Michelle was too busy to think about her next-door neighbor. But when Saturday rolled around, he was hard to ignore, trimming bushes and watering his lawn, wearing cargo shorts and Nittany Lions T-shirt.

With the thin cotton stretched tight across his back as he cut and pruned, it was obvious he had some serious muscles. Of course it wasn't as if Michelle was sitting out front in a lawn chair watching him. No, she was walking Sasha around the block while she waited for July Wahl.

July was a friend who'd been a photojournalist before getting into nature photography. She had an excellent eye and had been the first photographer Michelle had thought of when she and her partner had decided to update their website.

They wanted photos on the site to show them looking friendly and approachable. If anyone could make that happen, it would be July.

Michelle was just rounding the corner when she saw her friend pull into her driveway. She tried to hurry Sasha along but the dog would not be rushed. Just as she feared, by the time she reached the front of her house, July had walked over to speak with Gabe.

Ever since the After-Hours event Monday night, Michelle had tried to confine her interaction with her neighbor to a simple nod of the head.

"July," Michelle called to her friend as she drew close. "Thanks for coming over."

"My pleasure." The auburn-haired beauty looked stylish as always in yellow capris, a multi-colored scarf belt and white cotton shirt. "Gabe and I were just talking dogs. He owned a lot of different breeds growing up."

Yep, her neighbor was a true Renaissance man. Sexy. Great listener. Dog expert.

Michelle smiled.

"David and I've been discussing getting the boys a puppy," July said to Gabe. "Perhaps one of these times at The Coffee Pot you'll let us pick your brain about what breed might be a good match."

"Sure." Gabe's crooked smile encompassed Michelle. "It'd be my pleasure."

"Are you ready to go inside, July?" Michelle asked, feeling suddenly warm. "I'll make us some iced tea and get Sasha fresh water."

"It's good to see Sasha again." July reached over and gave the dog a pat on the head, then cocked her head. A tiny frown furrowed her brow. "Is it just me or is Sasha's coat not as thick? And she looks like she's lost weight."

Michelle saw the question—and the worry—in Gabe's eyes.

"I took her to the vet Tuesday." Michelle answered July but kept her gaze focused on Gabe. "Dr. Pitts did a thorough exam, ran a bunch of blood work and diagnosed her with hypothyroidism."

July's green eyes grew puzzled. "The hair loss fits that diagnosis, but don't you usually gain weight with that condition, instead of lose it?"

"Normally," Michelle admitted. "But some dogs become so lethargic they just don't feel like eating. To complicate matters, I'd recently switched Sasha to a food she ended up not liking."

"Thank God that's all it was," Gabe said and Michelle heard the relief in his voice.

After chatting with Gabe for a few more minutes, July followed Michelle inside. Once in the kitchen, Sasha ate the rest of the food in her dish, then looked up and whined.

Michelle smiled and patted the top of the dog's head. "You've had enough for now, sweetheart."

"Gabe sure seemed concerned about her." July leaned back against the counter, a speculative look in her eyes.

"He had a Golden who'd died of cancer." Michelle added fresh water to the dog bowl. "He worried Sasha might have the same thing."

July wanted to get right to work, so instead of enjoying a glass of iced tea, Michelle spent the next hour smiling for the camera in a variety of different outfits.

While July took the photos, Sasha padded

around the house, barking at a squirrel running across the back deck and playing with a fuzzy blue-and-white soccer ball. Seeing Sasha active again made Michelle want to laugh with pure joy.

After the session concluded, Michelle poured her and July a glass of iced tea and they headed to the back deck with a plate of peanut butter cookies. Of course, when they'd decided to sit outdoors, Michelle didn't know Gabe would be out in his yard tossing a softball back and forth with his daughter.

Even though she'd seen the teenager in passing, this was the first time Michelle had gotten a good look at her. Finley was tall with dark brown hair like her father, but her complexion was fair. From where Michelle sat she couldn't see the color of her eyes. The girl talked as much as she threw, the conversation with her father interspersed with laughter.

According to Lexi, Finley was a good-natured

girl and she and Addie were on their way to becoming the best of friends.

July cocked her head. "Did you hear a car drive up?"

The words had barely left her mouth when a car door slammed. Seconds later, the doorbell chimed.

"Looks like whoever it is came to see us." Michelle stood. "I'll check and be right back."

When she opened the front door, she saw David, July's husband. "This is a pleasant surprise."

"It's good to see you, again." David smiled. "I hope I'm not interrupting your session?"

Dressed in khaki shorts and a white polo shirt, Dr. David Wahl was a handsome, confident man with dark hair and piercing blue eyes.

"Actually we just recently finished and were enjoying some iced tea." Michelle motioned for him to follow her.

By the time they reached the back deck, July

was standing, a look of worry on her face. "I heard your voice. Are the boys okay?"

"They're fine." David leaned over and kissed his wife's cheek. "My parents took them to some event at the Children's Museum. They wanted to keep them overnight. I told them it was okay."

"I wonder why your mom didn't ask me?" July mused, puzzlement furrowing her brow. "She usually calls me for stuff like that."

"Reaching you might have been a little difficult considering this was at home." He pulled a tiny smartphone from his pocket and pressed it into her hands.

"Oops." July blushed. "Michelle and I were so busy I haven't even missed it. Thanks for bringing it to me."

"Would you like some iced tea, David?" Michelle asked. "Or a peanut butter cookie? They're homemade."

David glanced longingly at the platter of cookies. "Very tempting, but I actually wanted to see if July was interested in stopping for dinner on our way home."

July's expression turned thoughtful. She turned to Michelle. "Do you have plans for this evening?"

"No," Michelle said cautiously. "Why?"

Her friend clearly had something up her sleeve. While Michelle didn't know what it was, she had a feeling she would soon find out.

"We could grill. It's a beautiful evening. David could run to the store and get the steaks and beer." July's voice trembled with excitement. "You and I could whip up a salad while he's gone."

"Sounds good to me." David glanced at Michelle.

The last thing Michelle wanted was for July and David to feel sorry for her. She'd already planned to have a simple dinner, finish the book she'd been reading and go to bed early. Unless, of course, she got called out for a delivery.

"It does sound like fun, but this is your night without the kids." Michelle reminded her friends.

"You should spend it alone. Or with another couple. Not with me."

"Are you worried about being a third wheel?" July's voice rose. "Seriously?"

"If that's your concern," David exchanged a look with his wife. "I know how to remedy it."

Without saying another word, David headed down the deck steps and across the lawn with Sasha on his heels.

"What is he—" The words died in Michelle's throat as she watched him approach Gabe. "Dear God, tell me he's not going to invite him to join us."

July popped a piece of cookie in her mouth. "Looks like it."

Thankfully, from the way Gabe was shaking his head, it appeared he wasn't interested. Michelle expelled the breath she didn't realize she'd been holding. But her relief was short-lived.

David smiled and headed across the yard, calling over his shoulder. "Come over at six."

"What was that about?" July asked her husband

when he reached the deck, slanting a sideways glance at Michelle.

"I invited Gabe and his daughter to join us and they accepted," David said with a smug smile.

Gabe and his teenage daughter.

In her house.

Michelle swallowed a nervous laugh and realized feeling like a third wheel was now the least of her concerns.

## Chapter Four

"Put some of the brownies you baked this morning on a plate and we'll take them with us," Gabe said to his daughter.

Finley looked up from the kitchen table where she sat, book in hand. "I made those for us, not for them."

Gabe counted to ten and reminded himself that Finley had hoped for a different outcome for this evening. Yesterday she'd asked if she could invite Addie over tonight and he'd said yes. Unfortunately Addie already had plans. "Even though it will be only adults tonight, July is a photographer and I know you like that kind of stuff. Plus Sasha will be there."

Relief flooded Gabe when Finley's lips turned upward. His daughter had a deep love for dogs and this was something animals seemed to sense. Earlier Sasha had made a beeline across the yard to Finley.

"I still don't see why we have to give them our brownies." Finley pushed back her chair and stood. She glanced down at her denim skirt and top. "Or why I had to dress up."

Gabe slipped an arm around her shoulders and gave a squeeze. "They're giving us dinner. The least we can do is bring dessert. And if I had to change, so do you."

"We looked okay the way we were," Finley grumbled. "Or at least I did."

"Oh, so you're saying it was only me?" Gabe teased.

"No comment." Finley stepped back and looked him up and down, taking in his khaki pants and blue plaid shirt. "You look…pretty good. For an old guy, that is."

"I just turned thirty-one." He bristled with feigned outrage. "Hardly over-the-hill."

A smile lifted her lips. "Keep telling yourself that, old man."

Gabe chuckled, overcome with love for this child of his. He thought of the things her mother had been unwilling to give up. College life. Living on campus. Spring break trips.

Not for one minute did he regret the choice he made. He wondered if Shannon could say the same thing.

Impulsively he gave Finley a quick hug, planting a kiss on the top of her head.

"Hey," she twisted away. Her brows pulled together, but he saw the pleased look in her eyes. "What was that for?"

"I love you." The words came easily to his lips, the emotion as natural as breathing. "I'm proud of the trouper you've been during this move. I know it hasn't been easy."

"I'm a Davis." She pulled back her shoulders and straightened. "According to Grandpa, we do what needs to be done. And we don't whine."

*Thank you, Dad,* Gabe thought. His parents had been such positive role models for Finley.

"He's absolutely right. As always." Gabe pulled a paper plate from a drawer, along with some plastic wrap. "This should do for the brownies."

This time there wasn't a single grumble as Finley quickly washed her hands, then began transferring the chocolate squares to a disposable plate.

Gabe took a deep breath, feeling suddenly unsure about tonight's barbecue. He hoped accepting the dinner offer hadn't been a mistake.

"Do you like her?"

For a second Gabe wasn't sure he'd heard correctly. He turned toward Finley. "Who?"

"Michelle. Our neighbor," Finley clarified a bit impatiently. "Do you like her?"

"She seems nice." Gabe chose his words carefully, not wanting there to be any misunderstanding. "If you're asking if I want to date her, the answer is no."

Finley tilted her head. "Not your type?"

An image of Michelle flashed before him. A gorgeous blue-eyed blonde with long legs and big— Gabe cut off the thought. "She's okay. It's just I don't want to date anyone right now. This isn't a good time."

When he'd graduated with his degree in Construction Management, Gabe had thought long and hard about his next steps. Did he want to stay on the East Coast? Move to Florida where his parents now lived? Or head out west to a part of the country that had always appealed to him?

Finley was already in middle school, so it had been important to consider carefully. If they didn't relocate soon, she'd be in high school, which would make a move at that point difficult.

Wherever he ended up, Gabe was determined to secure a position that would not only allow him to advance in his career but also give him time for a rich and full home life.

He'd found that position with Joel Dennes's firm. Now that he and Finley were in Jackson Hole, his next step was to focus on getting comfortable in his new job as well as help his daughter acclimate to a different town. Those were his priorities. Six months from now, a year from now, there would be time to date.

He glanced at the clock. Five until six. "It's time. We don't want to be late."

Finley picked up the brownies. "Chill, Dad. They've probably already forgotten we're coming."

Michelle heard the doorbell just as the clock struck six. She hurried across the hardwood flooring, Sasha at her side.

She'd expected Gabe and his daughter to simply cut across the backyard. After all, David was already on the deck tending the grill, the delicious smell of steaks wafting in the air. Instead they'd gone to the front, like this was a big deal... which was how it felt.

Having two extra guests for dinner shouldn't have affected Michelle in the least. She liked to entertain and often had friends over.

But right now her chest felt as if a flock of hummingbirds had taken up residence. It was probably, she decided, because of Finley. How on earth were they going to entertain her? What did thirteen-year-olds even talk about?

Michelle opened the door. Sasha automatically sat. "Welcome."

"Thanks for inviting us." Gabe took hold of the screen door and motioned his daughter inside.

The girl had a plate of brownies in her hands. When Finley glanced in her direction Michelle realized that, unlike her father, the teen's eyes were a bright vivid blue.

"I'll put these on the kitchen counter." Finley started forward, but Gabe stopped her with a touch on her arm.

"First you need to meet our hostess," he said to his daughter in a gentle but firm voice. He quickly performed the introductions.

"It's nice to meet you, Dr. Kerns," Finley said in a soft, shy voice. "Thank you for inviting us to dinner."

"It's good to finally meet you, Finley. Please, call me Michelle." The dog at her feet whined. A smile lifted Michelle's lips. "I believe you've already met Sasha."

Finley handed her father the plate of brownies, then crouched down in front of the dog.

"Sasha, shake," Michelle ordered and the dog obligingly lifted one paw.

Finley took the paw, gave it a shake, then laughed, looking up at her dad.

A touching father-daughter moment, Michelle thought. Ed and his daughters had been close, too. A coldness filled her veins.

"Let me take these." Michelle lifted the brownies from Gabe's hands. "July and David are on the deck. Let's join them."

As they followed her through the home, she had to work to slow her breathing. She didn't know why she felt so jittery. After all, it wasn't as if she was interested in Gabe Davis.

Yet, for all her apprehension about the evening, once it got rolling, it couldn't have gone better. Finley played ball with the dog in the backyard while the adults socialized.

Gabe was charming. There was no other way for Michelle to say it. When David insisted he had the grilling under control, Gabe carried plates out to the table, grabbed condiments from the refrigerator and added cranberries to the salad.

"You seem comfortable in the kitchen," July commented when he scattered blue cheese crumbles over the top of the lettuce.

"Finley and I divide cooking duties," Gabe said with a smile. "My mother gave us some cooking lessons and tips on making nutritious meals on a budget. If not for her help, I'm afraid we'd be surviving on fast food."

"Does your mother live in Philadelphia?" Even though the conversation had been between July and Gabe, Michelle decided with only three of them in the kitchen, it was okay for her to jump into the conversation.

"My parents moved to Florida several years ago." Gabe finished with the salad, then turned those warm golden eyes in her direction. "We both hated to see them go."

Michelle grabbed steak sauce from the refrigerator and kept her tone offhand. "You were young when Finley was born.…"

"I turned eighteen a couple days before her birth," Gabe said.

"So your mother took care of her for you?" Michelle prompted when he didn't elaborate.

"My parents helped," Gabe acknowledged, "but they made it clear that Finley was my daughter, my responsibility, which is how I saw it, too."

"Because she was your mistake." The minute the words left her mouth, Michelle wished she could call them back. The truth was, she didn't see any child as a mistake. They were precious gifts from above. She'd devoted her career to bringing them safely into the world.

Gabe opened his mouth, then shut it.

"I'm sorry." Michelle started to reach out to him but pulled back, not wanting to be too familiar. Still, he needed to know where she stood. "That came out wrong. To me every child is a miracle, regardless of timing."

"She may not have been planned," Gabe said slowly as if she hadn't spoken, "but Finley was a great gift."

"I gave birth to our oldest son," July confided, "before David and I were married. Even though the timing might not be what some would consider perfect, I believe that was how it was meant to be. Adam came into our lives according to a higher timetable, not according to mine."

The smile Gabe directed at July was warm. But when he shifted his gaze to Michelle, there was a coolness in his eyes that hadn't been there moments before. "Perhaps one day—when you have a child of your own—you'll understand."

It was a low blow, but she figured she deserved it. "As I said, I'm sorry. It came out wrong." Michelle forced a smile to her lips. "I think we're ready to eat."

By the time they took their seats around the wooden table on the deck, Michelle concluded that inviting Gabe and Finley over had been a mistake. One she wouldn't repeat.

Despite the fact that her two neighbors were perfect guests, Michelle continued to feel off balanced. That insensitive comment she'd uttered in the kitchen was a perfect example of her jumbled thoughts.

"I really like photography," she overheard Finley say to July. "But I'm not very good at it."

"What kind of camera do you have?" July asked.

"A cheap digital." Finley glanced at her father. "I asked for a better one for my birthday, but we didn't have the money."

"Moving across the country isn't cheap." Gabe cut off a bite of steak. "Not to mention spending seven hundred dollars for a birthday present isn't something I'd ever consider appropriate."

"Ah, Dad," Finley began but stopped when her eyes met her father's. She cleared her throat and focused on the others around the table. "I'm hoping to earn the money this summer. So if you know of anyone who needs a babysitter—I've completed the Red Cross certification—or have odd jobs I could do, please let me know."

July put down her fork and turned to Michelle. "Didn't you say something during book club about wishing you had someone to walk Sasha during the day?"

"I could walk her," Finley began almost before the words left July's mouth. "Because I live next door, Dad wouldn't have to drive me or anything. Whenever you needed me, I'd be available."

Michelle remembered being thirteen and eager to work, but too young for a work permit. And Finley was right, with her living next door, it couldn't be any more perfect. But to have such a close association with Gabe's daughter...

"Do you need someone, Doctor, I mean Michelle?" Finley pressed, her voice quivering with excitement.

"Honey." Gabe placed a hand on his daughter's shoulder when Michelle didn't immediately respond. "Michelle may already have someone in mind."

He'd generously given her an out, but this time she wasn't going to take it. What did it matter whose child Finley was? It wasn't as if Michelle and Gabe were *dating*. It certainly wasn't as if she'd ever consider *marrying* him.

"If you're serious, I'd like to take you up on your offer, Finley." Michelle's smile widened as Finley squealed. "After supper we can talk about the specifics."

"Ohmygosh, thank you so much." The words tumbled from Finley's mouth. "I'll take good care of her. I promise."

Of that Michelle had no doubt. "I know you will. I wouldn't trust Sasha's care to just anyone."

Across Finley's head, Gabe's eyes caught hers.

"Thank you," he mouthed and a rush of warmth flowed through her veins.

*No big deal,* she told herself, taking another bite of salad. This was strictly a business arrangement between her and Finley. It didn't have a thing to do with making Gabe happy. Not one thing.

Gabe had assumed he'd see Michelle at church on Sunday, but she wasn't there or at breakfast afterward. He'd forgiven her for her comment about Finley being a mistake. There had been times in his past when he'd put his foot in his mouth, too. He believed her apology had been sincere.

He'd hoped for some private time to tell her that and to thank her for giving Finley the dog-walking job. Between taking care of Sasha and her new friendship with Addie, the summer was shaping up quite nicely for his daughter.

His days had begun to fill up as well. During breakfast, David had asked him about serving on a committee for the chamber of commerce. Even though developing a veterans memorial garden was a worthy task, apparently David was having difficulty coming up with committee members.

Gabe was amazed by the energy in the Jackson Hole Chamber of Commerce. There were so many committees and projects that he felt like a slacker for not being involved in one yet. In Philly, he'd belonged but rarely attended. Here it was part of the social and professional fabric of the community.

Joel wholeheartedly supported his involvement, especially because he'd recently backed off his own volunteer efforts. But serving on the committee didn't mean Gabe could neglect his other job duties. He'd spent all morning on the phone lining up subcontractors for a house they were building near Moose and ordering materials for another job in the mountains. He'd waited until Finley left to take Sasha for a walk before heading downtown.

Even though traffic seemed heavier than normal, Gabe easily found a parking space on the street not far from the coffee shop. He checked his phone before stepping out of the truck, pleased to see his afternoon meeting had confirmed. He was going over the blueprints with some new clients for a home they were building in the Spring Gulch subdivision. But that appointment wasn't until two o'clock. That gave him a good two hours until he needed to get on the road. Surely the planning meeting wouldn't take that long.

Hill of Beans had a line at the counter, but Gabe saw Adrianna Lee had secured a large round table toward the front of the store. Gabe had been introduced to Adrianna, the midwife who worked with Michelle, at the After-Hours event. The dark-haired beauty wasn't a woman any red-blooded male would easily forget.

With her thick chestnut hair, green bedroom eyes and pouty lips, she reminded him of a Brazilian actress whose name he couldn't quite recall.

Gabe ordered a sandwich and a cola, then

brought them with him to the table. "May I join you?"

A look of relief skittered across Adrianna's face. "I'm glad to see you. For a second I thought this was going to end up being a meeting of one."

He noticed she'd grabbed a small salad and was dipping her fork into the dressing. Barely enough to feed a bird and a far cry from Michelle's hearty appetite.

"Who else is coming?" Gabe pulled out a chair and took a seat.

"Yours was the only name David gave me. But he said to plan on four or five, so I got a large table. I feel foolish sitting here with people looking for places to sit."

"We weren't starting until 11:30." Gabe picked up his phone and glanced at it. "Which is now."

"They may simply be running late," Adrianna said. "I'm off today, so getting here early wasn't a problem. If they don't show, I guess we can do the meeting without them."

"I didn't receive any specifics on the project."

Gabe glanced at the portfolio on the table next to Adrianna. "Do you have anything with you?"

Adrianna's eyes widened. "I thought David gave you the information."

"I can tell this is going to be a productive meeting." Gabe chuckled.

Adrianna's echoing laughter disappeared in a sharp intake of air.

Because she was facing the line at the counter, he assumed the others they'd been expecting— the ones who really knew what was going on— had shown up.

"Are they here?" Gabe turned in his seat. "You'll have to point them out to me—"

Whatever he'd been about to say died in his throat when he saw the two at the counter. "Are Tripp and Michelle on our committee?"

Gabe wasn't sure if he wanted the answer to be yes or no.

Adrianna slowly shook her head. "I think they're on a date."

Her lilting voice was soft and controlled, but with an undercurrent of tension.

"Wouldn't surprise me," Gabe said, remembering Tripp putting his arm around her at the After-Hours event.

The two picked up their food, then scanned the room, obviously looking for a place to sit. When Michelle's gaze fell on him, Gabe motioned to her.

Adrianna's smile appeared frozen on her lips.

"They can't sit with us," she hissed, her smile never wavering.

"They can until our other committee members arrive." Even though he understood Adrianna's reluctance, he couldn't let friends wander around searching for a place to sit when they had spots open at their table.

As they wove their way through the tables, Gabe noted that Michelle's sleeveless navy dress made her look completely professional, giving little hint of the curves beneath the fabric. Tripp wore a suit and, unlike the other night, he'd kept the jacket on this time.

"What a surprise." Michelle glanced from him to Adrianna. "I didn't realize you two even knew each other."

"You introduced us at the After-Hours event," Gabe reminded her.

"Gabe and I are going to be working on the veterans memorial garden project for the chamber of commerce," Adrianna said quickly, her gaze darting between Tripp and Michelle.

"Just the two of you?" Tripp cocked his head. "Big committee."

"There's supposed to be at least four of us." Adrianna shifted in her seat. "But David didn't give us their names."

"And they haven't showed." Gabe rose to his feet and pulled out a chair for Michelle. "Please join us."

"Yes," Adrianna echoed, her cheeks slightly flushed. "Please do."

"Because you asked so nicely—" Tripp's smile was directed at her alone "—how can I refuse?"

Adrianna's color deepened.

"Your other committee members may simply be running late." Michelle placed her tray on the table and sat down. "If they show up, Tripp and I will find another spot to sit."

"Speak for yourself." Tripp plopped into the chair next to Adrianna. "I like where I'm sitting."

"Tell us about the veterans memorial garden project." Michelle stabbed a forkful of dill potato salad but kept her gaze focused on Gabe. "Sounds interesting."

"You and Tripp should join the committee, Michi," Adrianna surprised Gabe by offering, the words tumbling from her pouty lips. "We could muddle through this together."

"Muddle?" Tripp's eyes took on a devilish gleam. "Sounds like my kind of project."

"We're not sure what it involves," Gabe admitted. "But it's a worthy cause."

"It should be fun." Adrianna's gaze shifted to

Michelle. "Especially for us, because we both like gardens."

"I'm interested." Tripp dipped his spoon into his bowl of soup. "My father is a Vietnam veteran. I know that having a memorial garden to honor veterans of all the eras would please him. I only hope he'll be around to see its completion."

"How is your dad doing?" Adrianna placed her hand lightly on Tripp's forearm.

"Okay." The look of pain in Tripp's eyes said otherwise.

"If there's ever anything I can do—" Adrianna began.

Tripp smiled his thanks, then shifted his attention to Gabe. "I'll let David know when I see him at the hospital that Michelle and I are interested in serving on the committee."

"Good." Gabe slanted a sideways glance at Michelle. "What brings the two of you to Hill of Beans today?"

Michelle smiled as if she found his question amusing. "Isn't it obvious? We came for lunch.

After we eat, I'm going to do some quick shopping before heading back to the clinic."

"Do you have a special occasion that you're shopping for?" Adrianna dipped her fork into the salad dressing and cocked her head.

"A dress for Travis and Mary Karen's party on Saturday," Michelle told her. "I'm sure I have something that would work, but I'm in the mood for a new outfit."

Gabe took a sip of cola. "Joel told me the party is an annual event and lots of fun."

"It's one of *the* social events of the summer," Michelle confirmed. "I wouldn't miss it."

Tripp nodded. "I'll be there."

Gabe's settled his gaze on Adrianna, who sat quietly sipping her tea. "What about you?"

"No invitation." Adrianna spoke in a matter-of-fact tone, her eyes giving nothing away.

Michelle reached across the table and covered her friend's hand with hers. "That had to be an oversight. I'll talk to Mary Karen and—"

"Please don't." Bright patches of pink dotted Adrianna's cheeks. "It's not a big deal."

"Go with me." Tripp met her gaze. "As my plus one."

Adrianna shook her head and politely demurred.

"We could all go together." Michelle glanced around the table. "It'll be fun. C'mon, Anna. Say you'll do it."

Still the midwife hesitated until Tripp clasped her hand in his. "Please say you'll come. It won't be the same without you."

Frankly, Gabe thought the begging was overkill, but a smile immediately lifted Adrianna's full lips.

"Because you put it that way, how can I refuse?"

Tripp leaned forward. For a second it appeared he was going to kiss the dark-haired beauty, but he pulled back at the last minute.

An awkward silence descended over the table.

Michelle glanced at her watch and gave a little

yelp. "No time for shopping today. I need to get to the clinic."

"What time—" Adrianna glanced at the clock on the wall. "Oh, my goodness, I didn't realize it was so late. I have a hair appointment."

Both women pushed back their chairs and stood.

Gabe and Tripp rose to their feet at the same time.

"If you want, I'll see what I can find out from David about the project and we can talk later tonight," Michelle said to Gabe.

Adrianna's curious gaze darted from her friend to Gabe. Michelle's face colored.

"Gabe has the adjacent townhome," Michelle explained. "It's inevitable that we see each other."

*Inevitable.* Gabe liked the sound of that.

As the two women hurried off, Gabe realized this was one meeting that far exceeded his expectations.

## *Chapter Five*

Michelle had barely walked through her front door that evening when Betsy called asking what she should bring. Until that moment Michelle had forgotten that Book Club had reverted to its normal Monday night schedule and tonight's meeting was at her house. Thankfully, as was the custom, each of her friends would bring something for dinner.

Lexi, the closest to a gourmet cook the group had, was charged with bringing the entrée. She'd chosen a ham, spinach and onion quiche. Betsy brought a dandelion and frisée salad. Michelle pulled out the crusty bread that she'd gotten at the bakery yesterday. July, a busy mom of two little boys, brought a caramel apple pie she'd picked up at a local bakery. And Mary Karen, mother of five, brought several bottles of wine.

Michelle wondered if Gabe would have stopped over if the women hadn't been arriving when he'd driven up. She'd given him a friendly wave, then hurried inside with her friends.

After eating, the book club members moved the discussion out to the deck. Although they predominantly read fiction, for this week the book was *The Politics of Aristotle.*

Michelle had found it a little dry, but had gotten through it by reading Sasha to sleep.

"No more ancient Greeks for a long time," Mary Karen said in the same no-nonsense tone she used to control her rambunctious boys. She took a big sip of wine. "Reading that book was pure torture."

"I liked it." July paused, then wrinkled her nose. "Sort of."

"It made me think." Lexi lifted a glass of wine to her lips, a thoughtful expression on her pretty face.

"Do we really have to prolong the torture by talking about that stupid book?" Mary Karen's normally upbeat and cheerful voice stopped just short of a whine.

"I usually like stuff like this," Betsy said hesitantly. Like Michelle, the legal assistant was a relatively new book club member. "But I agree with Mary Karen. Talking about it would only prolong the torture."

"It's a book club." July glanced around the table. "We can't simply sit here and gossip."

"Sure we can," her sister-in-law Mary Karen interrupted.

July shook her head. "No, we can't. We need to talk about something book-related."

"How about the qualities we like to see in a male protagonist?" Michelle suggested.

"Good suggestion." Lexi gave an approving nod.

"Works for me," Betsy said.

"Okay," July agreed.

"I know what I like to see." Mary Karen raised her hand and waved it in the air like she was in school waiting for the teacher to call on her.

As the hostess, Michelle was the discussion leader for the evening. She smiled at the petite blonde. "What's the quality?"

"A sense of humor." Mary Karen's lips quirked upward. "Travis always makes me laugh. If the protagonist has a sense of humor, I almost always fall in love with him."

"I agree." Betsy's gaze turned dreamy. "Travis is like my Ryan. I never know what he's going to say."

"Intelligence is a real turn-on for me," Lexi mused, "with a hint of mystery."

"A man you can depend on and trust. His word should mean something," July added, her green eyes serious.

Mary Karen leaned forward, resting her arms on the table, her gaze focused on Michelle. "What do you like?"

"Are we discussing men in books?" A nervous

laugh slipped past Michelle's lips. "Or a flesh-and-blood male?"

"It's kind of hard to separate the two." Lexi's expression was surprisingly serious. "I think the men we're drawn to in the pages of books are the type of men we hope to find someday or they remind us of the man we've already found."

"All of the qualities you've mentioned are good ones." Michelle lifted her hand and counted off on her fingers. "Sense of humor, intelligence, trustworthy and dependable. I'd also add sexual attraction."

"Oh my, yes." Mary Karen pretended to fan herself. The other women laughed.

"That's why description in a book is vital," Michelle continued. "I have to be able to see the protagonist in my mind to know if I'm attracted to him."

"Or you could simply look next door." July's lips quirked up in an impish smile. Once again the other women laughed.

"Gabe Davis is hot," Betsy said. "Not as cute as my Ryan but hot."

"What do you think of him, Michelle?" Lexi gazed at Michelle through lowered lashes. "Do you find your neighbor sexy?"

"He's got the look that I like," Michelle reluctantly admitted.

"Which is?" Mary Karen prompted.

"Dark hair. Tall." Michelle paused. "With some serious muscles."

"So are you and Gabe dating?"

Michelle wasn't sure which one of her friends asked the question. Did it really even matter? The fact was, she could tell by the look in their eyes that they all wanted to know the answer.

"We're just neighbors." Michelle glanced down at Sasha sleeping beside her feet. "I often see him, mostly coming and going. And his daughter, Finley, is now walking Sasha for me while I'm at work."

"I heard you had lunch with him at Hill of Beans today." Betsy slid her book into her purse as if declaring they'd moved on to a different topic.

"Sounds like a date to me." A twinkle danced in July's eyes. "And to think we're the last to know."

"Actually Tripp and I went there to grab a quick lunch. We ran into Gabe and Adrianna. They're on a committee for the chamber of commerce dealing with the veterans memorial garden project." Michelle stopped her nervous chatter and fixed her gaze to Mary Karen. "The four of us decided to attend your summer solstice party together. You don't care if we bring Adrianna, do you?"

"Didn't she get an invitation?" Mary Karen's blond brows pulled together. "She was on the list."

"So the four of you are going together." Lexi brought a finger to her lips. "Which of those two handsome men is going to be *your* plus one?"

"Anyone want more pie?" Michelle asked, experiencing a sudden desire to return to her hostess duties.

"I know which one will be her date," July said.

Everyone at the table focused their attention on July, including Michelle.

"She said men with dark hair turn her on, right?" July smiled. "That means Gabe Davis is her man."

Was Gabe Davis her man? Did she want him to be? Those questions kept running through Michelle's mind Saturday while she got ready for the party.

She'd assumed they'd all ride together. Wasn't that what *all going together* meant? Then Tripp had called and said it would work better if he could simply swing by and pick up Adrianna. The two of them would meet her and Gabe there. Michelle had been so stunned that she hadn't known what to say except okay.

Even though Adrianna hadn't said much this past week, Michelle knew the midwife was looking forward to the party. She wondered how much of Anna's excitement had to do with the fact that Tripp was picking her up?

Michelle had mixed feelings about spending so much alone time with Gabe. She'd already confessed to her book club that Gabe had the look she liked. But he also had something that made him off-limits for anything more than a simple friendship—a teenage daughter.

Because of this, she had to continue to think of Gabe as simply a neighbor giving her a ride to the party. Changing her clothes three times hadn't a thing to do with wanting to impress him. Because there would be lots of old friends as well as new people to meet, Michelle merely wanted to ensure she looked her best.

She added a dab of gloss on top of her red lipstick and smiled into the mirror, liking the reflection. The black wrap dress might not be new, but she hadn't been able to find anything in any store that she liked better.

The soft fabric caressed her skin and the cut of

the dress emphasized her lean but curvy figure. Glittery earrings dangled from her ears and she'd donned a pair of strappy silver sandals.

Sasha lifted her head as Michelle entered the living room. An assessing look filled the dog's dark eyes before she wagged her tail, giving Michelle the golden retriever seal of approval.

"Thanks for the vote of confidence, sweetie." Michelle reached down and patted the dog's silky head.

Despite her trepidation over attending the party with Gabe, Michelle experienced a shiver of anticipation. She loved parties, both giving and attending them.

That was something she'd learned about herself since moving to Jackson Hole. Before that, she'd been too busy with school even to think about book clubs, barbecues and parties. But the friends she'd made since moving here had shown her that socializing could be fun.

The bell rang and when Michelle pulled open the door, not only Gabe stood there, but Finley, as well. Michelle hid her surprise behind a broad welcoming smile.

"Come in." She stepped aside to let them enter.

Even though Gabe was dressed for a party in dark pants and a gray shirt that hugged his muscular chest, she wondered if Finley being with him meant his plans for the evening had changed.

"You're probably wondering why this beautiful young lady is with me." Gabe shot his daughter a conspiratorial wink.

"Um." Michelle decided to play along. She placed a finger to her lips. "You need a chaperone?"

"Good one." Gabe laughed. "Actually Mary Karen called. One of the babysitters they had for the little kids cancelled at the last minute. Finley agreed to take that girl's place."

Michelle smiled at Finley, who looked party-ready in a simple blue dress with ballet flats.

She wasn't surprised that Mary Karen had hired sitters for the party. The families in their social circle always appreciated being able to bring their children with them. "That was nice of you to help her out on short notice."

Finley looked up from petting Sasha. "She needed someone and I was available," the girl said in a matter-of-fact tone. "I'm hoping I'll get called for other parties."

"I'm sure you will." Gabe spoke decisively with a father's confidence. "Especially once they see how good you are with children."

Finley straightened and glanced at her watch. "I told Mary Karen I'd try to get there as soon as possible."

Michelle couldn't help but admire the girl's sense of responsibility. She shot her an approving smile. Still, as Michelle grabbed her bag from the side table, disappointment began to wrap itself around her heart.

She should be relieved at having a third party in the car. Thankful she didn't have to spend endless minutes on the drive to the mountains with only Gabe. Instead she felt surprisingly resentful over having to share his attention.

It was then Michelle admitted to herself that a tiny part of her had been looking forward to getting to know Gabe better. And that tiny part was actually bummed over the change in plans. Which considering the importance of keeping her distance from Gabe, made no sense at all.

The first thing Gabe noticed when they walked through the door of Travis and Mary Karen's new home in the mountains surrounding Jackson was the mistletoe hanging above his head.

He might have missed it if he hadn't been so intent on inspecting the foyer. Joel had told him that his company had built this home and Gabe was eager to inspect the details. Outside he'd admired the red cedar siding of the rambling two-story dwelling and the sturdy porch. When Travis had ushered them inside, Gabe had taken note of the quarry-tiled entry—easy to keep clean when you had five small children—and ceilings coffered with rough-hewn beams.

It was when Gabe's eyes were drawn upward

in admiration of those sturdy beams that he noticed the mistletoe. He turned to Travis—Mary Karen had hustled Finley off before his daughter's feet had even hit the tile—and gestured toward the sprig of evergreen leaves and white berries. "What's up with that?"

Travis didn't even pretend to not understand. Beside him, Michelle lifted her gaze upward.

"My wife and I share fond memories of times under the mistletoe," Travis said quite seriously, though a devilish gleam lit his eyes. "We decided it'd be fun to help our friends start building some of their own memories."

"Wasn't Christmas six months ago?" Gabe kept his tone light.

"Once a year just isn't enough." Travis's gaze shifted to Michelle before returning to Gabe. He cocked his head. "Would you and Michelle like the honor of being the first couple to take advantage of this particular sprig of mistletoe?"

Was Travis really asking—*encouraging*—him to kiss Michelle?

For a second Gabe wondered what the pretty doctor would do if he pulled her into his arms and did just that, simply for the heck of it?

As if she could read his thoughts, Michelle's eyes widened. She took a step back.

"No pressure." Travis chuckled. "You'll find mistletoe throughout the house, so if you're not in the mood now, there will be other opportunities."

"Such the consummate host." Michelle's sugary sweet tone couldn't hide her sarcasm. "You've thought of everything."

Travis appeared to find her resistance amusing.

"We aim to please." He grinned and rocked back on the heels of his cowboy boots. "Trust me, kissing turns a pleasant evening into something memorable."

Before Travis could say more, a curly-haired blond boy that looked about seven raced up and skidded to a stop in front of him.

"What are you doing here, Caleb?" Travis affectionately ruffled the child's hair, taking any sting from the words. "You should be downstairs playing with the other kids."

"You've got to come, Daddy. Mommy is super-mad."

Even though the child's voice trembled, Travis didn't appear overly concerned. With five children, Gabe guessed "Mommy being super-mad" was probably an everyday occurrence in the Fisher household. "What happened, Cal?"

"Connor dropped—" the boy hesitated, then swallowed hard "—a piece of cake into the fish tank."

"In *my* aquarium?" Travis's voice rose and his affable expression disappeared. The determined gleam in his eyes gave him the look of a man capable of controlling, er, parenting, a whole herd of young children.

The boy reluctantly nodded. "I told Connor fishes don't like that stuff, but he didn't believe me."

Travis raked a hand through his hair. He took a deep breath, then slowly let it out. He slanted a sideways glance at Gabe and Michelle before refocusing on his son. "Tell Mommy I'll be there in a minute."

Gabe met Travis's worried gaze. "If you need to take care of the...situation, don't hesitate on our account."

"Absolutely. Make sure your fish are okay," Michelle urged.

Travis shot them a grateful look before hurrying after his son.

Michelle shook her head. "I wouldn't want to be there when Travis sees globs of frosting and chunks of cake floating in his aquarium."

Gabe grimaced. "Poor Connor."

"He *did* put cake in a fish tank," Michelle reminded him.

"Finley once put a cup of grape juice in the washing machine with my white shirts." Gabe shook his head. "Kids do crazy things sometimes."

"True." Michelle took a few steps forward and paused at the edge of the living room. Tibetan rugs and oversize furniture brought a warm and cozy feel to the large-scale room. "My nephew once fed their cat ex-lax."

Gabe could visualize the resulting scene and it wasn't pretty. Still he had to ask. "How did that turn out?"

Michelle laughed. "Just as you'd expect."

"Compared to that, the grape juice really wasn't such a big deal." Gabe chuckled and realized he was enjoying the conversation. Perhaps because of being a single parent and so involved in his daughter's life, he enjoyed sharing kid stories. "How many nieces and nephews do you have?"

"Three," Michelle murmured, her gaze shifting to the room filled with people. "Looks like a good turnout."

The hum of conversation interspersed with laughter filled the air. Most of the men were dressed casually, although Gabe didn't see any in jeans. The women seemed to have gone to a little more effort, wearing dresses and heels and necklaces that glittered in the light.

Michelle's dress hugged her curves and the length made her legs look as if they went on forever. She'd left her hair down for the evening, but had pulled the strands back from her face with a thin black headband.

Gabe hadn't been sure how Michelle would react about Finley riding with them, but she'd been gracious. He'd appreciated the way she'd chatted with Finley, although she might have gone a bit overboard with making the child feel welcome.

She'd barely spoken five words to him on the way to the party. Not that he'd noticed. Or cared. It wasn't as if they were on a date. They were simply two neighbors sharing a ride to an event. And that's the way he wanted to keep it. "Isn't that Tripp and Adrianna by the buffet table?"

Michelle glanced in the direction he pointed. "Figures Tripp would be by the food."

"Shall we go say hello?" The second the words left his lips, Gabe had to stifle a groan. Hadn't he just gotten through reminding himself they weren't here as a couple? "I mean, I'm going to say hello."

She lifted one hand acknowledging Adrianna's wave. "I'll go with you."

As they made their way across the room, Gabe resisted the urge to rest his hand against her back. The resolve lasted until a waiter carrying a wooden serving tray got too close, causing Michelle to stumble.

Automatically Gabe reached out and pulled her close. He held her perhaps a second or two longer than necessary, but he told himself he simply wanted to make sure she'd fully regained her balance before he let her go.

By the time he finally released her, a becoming pink colored Michelle's cheeks.

"Thank you." Her voice sounded as unsteady as her feet had been only moments before.

Gabe kept his hand against the small of her back…just in case she lost her balance again. He took a deep breath, inhaling her clean, fresh scent. "You're wearing a different perfume tonight."

She tilted her head, a puzzled look in her eyes.

"You usually smell like flowers." He spoke quickly realizing they would soon reach Tripp and Adrianna. "Now you smell like pillowcases that have been hung out on a clothesline."

"It's called Fresh Linen." Michelle's blue eyes met his. "I'm surprised you noticed."

"There's very little I don't notice," he said with a wry smile, "especially about a beautiful woman."

## Chapter Six

"Anna." Michelle gave her friend a quick hug, trying to forget Gabe's words. *Beautiful.* He thought she was beautiful. But even Gabe would have to admit Michelle didn't hold a candle to her stunning friend. She held Adrianna at arm's length. "You look fabulous. Where did you find that dress?"

Adrianna smoothed an imaginary wrinkle from the green knit halter dress with a graceful, elegant hand. "I picked it up at Plumberry."

"I love that boutique." Michelle glanced at the

man standing at her side. "Doesn't she look fabulous, Gabe?"

He obligingly focused on the statuesque brunette. "Very nice."

"Green is definitely Adrianna's color," Tripp agreed.

Michelle half expected Gabe to say more about the dress, but his gaze was now on the long linen-clad table. "Quite a spread, though I'm not sure I could identify half of what I'm seeing."

"Lexi did the catering," Michelle informed the men. "That guarantees everything will be delicious."

Gabe's brows furrowed. "I thought she was a social worker."

"She is," Michelle said, "but she's also a gourmet cook."

Gabe gestured to the table. "And I suppose you know what all these…items are."

"Be careful, Davis," Tripp warned. "She'll think you're some hick from the sticks."

"Okay, tell me, smart guy, what are these?"

Gabe pointed to golden brown appetizers artistically displayed on what Michelle recognized as a floral-and-coral majolica plate.

Tripp leaned close and studied them for several seconds. One shoulder lifted in a slight shrug.

Gabe turned to Michelle, a smug look on his face.

She'd been watching the two men and trying hard not to smile. Mary Karen and Travis should have forgotten the gourmet food. Put a slab of ribs and some ears of corn in front of these two and they'd have been happy.

"Those are Rofumo cheese croquettes. Delicious," Michelle proclaimed, glancing at Adrianna.

"They're incredibly yummy," the brunette confirmed.

"A croquette?" Gabe looked so thoroughly confused that Michelle had to laugh.

While she and Gabe were talking, Tripp tugged Adrianna's arm. They stepped over to speak with Mr. Stromberg, the retired hospital administrator whom Tripp had replaced. Once again Michelle was left alone with Gabe.

"Rofumo is a semi-soft cheese smoked over hickory wood." Michelle picked up one of the croquettes. "To make this type of croquette, you take Idaho potatoes and Rofumo cheese, roll them in Italian breading, then flash fry and bake them."

"Sounds like it could be good," he said cautiously.

"See for yourself. Open up." Michelle held out the croquette and urged him to take a bite. But when his mouth closed over the appetizer, he caught the side of her fingers with his lips. She slowly pulled her hand back.

His gaze sought hers at the surprisingly intimate touch. Michelle ignored the backflips her heart was doing, picked up one for herself and took a bite.

A tad messy, she decided, feeling the cheese on her lips. It was her last rational thought as Gabe's mouth closed over hers.

The warm sweet kiss sent a shower of tingles raining all the way to the tips of her toes. When it was over she brought two fingers to her lips and tried to remember how to breathe. "What was that for?"

Her voice sounded shaky, even to her own ears.

Gabe cast a pointed glance upward.

Michelle tilted her head back and followed his gaze. Directly over them were a few dark waxy leaves interspersed with white berries. "Mistletoe?"

"I want this evening to be memorable."

His hands rested on her arms and the heat from his body urged her closer. The scent of his cologne enveloped her and everything—and everyone—around them disappeared until there was only her...and Gabe.

Gabe, the man with the thirteen-year-old daughter.

The realization wasn't quite a splash of cold water, but it was enough to make Michelle stop from lifting a hand to caress his cheek.

"Nothing has changed," she murmured, unable to pull her gaze from his face. She wasn't sure which one of them she was trying to convince. "We're still just neighbors. I'm not looking for more."

"I'm not either," he said in a husky rumble. "But you have to admit the kiss was pleasant."

*Pleasant?* Michelle didn't know whether to be insulted or amused by such a mundane term. "It wasn't bad," she said when she realized he expected a response. "For a first time."

For a first time? For the absolute *last* time.

Dear God, what kind of mixed signals was she giving out? It was as if her brain had gone on hiatus and decided to let her body call the shots.

"You've never been kissed before?" Gabe asked.

"What?" Michelle yanked her thoughts back to the present. "Of course I've been kissed before."

Surely her technique wasn't *that* horrible. Larry never seemed to have any complaints. Of course

Larry had probably been too busy thinking about being whipped to worry about how she kissed.

"You said this was your first time." Even though Gabe's eyes twinkled, he somehow managed to keep a straight face. "Sweet thirtysomething and never been kissed."

Michelle rolled her eyes.

"I must say for a first timer, you show great potential." He cupped her elbow and guided her away from the buffet table. "I think you'd be a quick study."

"And I suppose you'd be interested in tutoring me?"

"It could be fun." His gaze dropped to her lips, then farther down to linger at the hint of cleavage.

Her breasts began to tingle and an ache began low in her abdomen. Desire coursed through her veins like warm honey.

"Unfortunately, we've already decided that we're simply friends."

"Neighbors." She pushed the word past stiff lips.

"Although we're physically compatible—"

"—we won't be going down that road." Michelle straightened her shoulders and felt her brain finally take firm control of the situation.

"Absolutely not."

Even though he was merely confirming her sentiment, Michelle felt a twinge of irritation. She understood her reasons for dismissing him, but what possible reason could he have for not wanting to be involved with her?

Michelle had planned to attend church the next morning, but a patient Adrianna was handling unexpectedly needed a cesarean section and Michelle was called to the hospital.

After the delivery, she and Adrianna met at Hill of Beans to celebrate the birth of Jackson Hole's newest citizen. Feeling reckless, Michelle ordered a mocha frappé and even let them top it with whipped cream. Adrianna had her usual, a cup of black coffee.

Even though Michelle hadn't thought anyone

had seen Gabe kiss her, Adrianna brought up the subject only seconds after they settled at a table by the window.

"Blame it on the mistletoe," Michelle told her, which was absolutely true, at least in theory. She went on to emphasize Travis's comments at the front door and Gabe's original comment after the kiss.

"That's why he kissed you?" Adrianna's voice rose. "Because he wanted to make the evening memorable?"

"Those were his exact words," Michelle said with a rueful smile. "The funny thing is, it worked. I haven't been able to forget that night."

*Or the way I felt when his lips closed over mine.*

Adrianna drew an imaginary figure eight on the tabletop with her finger. "Was it awkward afterward?"

"Not really. Everyone was kissing everyone." Okay, perhaps that was an exaggeration, but Michelle had seen more than a handful of couples kissing during the course of the evening. "Those sprigs of mistletoe were everywhere."

"Tripp didn't try to kiss me."

"Tripp Randall is a gentleman," Michelle pointed out.

Adrianna sighed. "I guess."

Michelle dipped a spoon into the mile-high whipped topping and glanced at her friend. "Do you think you and Tripp will start dating?"

Adrianna clasped her fingers around the coffee cup. She stared into the dark liquid as if it contained tea leaves that could foretell her future. "No."

"Well, that was definitive." Michelle lifted a brow. "How can you be so sure?"

"I was his wife's friend."

"Her *high school* friend," Michelle reminded her for what felt like the zillionth time. "That was ages ago. Another century. I don't see what that has to do with now."

"It wasn't just back in high school. Gayle and I

kept in touch," Adrianna asserted. "That makes a relationship with Tripp awkward."

"But not impossible." Normally Michelle wouldn't be this pushy. After all, she didn't like people messing in her business and she tried to respect her friend's privacy. But she knew Anna liked Tripp.

"Even if you don't consider his family's prominence in the community, Tripp has a high-profile position as the administrator of the largest hospital in the area." A shutter dropped over Adrianna's green eyes. "We'd both bring a lot of baggage into a relationship."

Michelle wasn't sure what the prominence of Tripp's position had to do with anything. Or what baggage Adrianna was talking about. The midwife had never been married and had no children. Unless she was referring—for the zillionth and one time—to that long-ago friendship with Tripp's deceased wife.

"You know best." Michelle decided to let the

subject drop. For now. "It just seems like you two would be a good fit."

Adrianna's eyes took on a faraway look. "Trust me, it wouldn't work, so it's best not to even go there."

"At least you two can still be friends."

"I've begun to realize friendship comes with its own set of challenges." Adrianna leaned back in her chair, looking incredibly weary. "Is that what you and Gabe are...friends?"

Michelle thought for a moment. "More like friendly neighbors."

The look in Adrianna's eyes was clearly skeptical. "I don't recall ever kissing any of my neighbors."

Up until last night, Michelle hadn't either. But then again she'd never had a neighbor like Gabe. If only he didn't have Finley....

Almost immediately Michelle railed against the uncharitable thought. Especially because Finley had been nothing but nice and she'd found herself liking the girl. It would be so easy to forget her reservations....

The second the temptation rose, Michelle shoved it down. Ed's daughters had seemed nice, too. Until they'd realized things were heating up between her and their dad. That's when their little claws had come out. "The kiss was just a one-time thing."

"Says who?"

"Gabe and I discussed it. We decided it wouldn't happen again."

Adrianna's lips quirked upward.

"Why are you looking at me like that?"

"If it was simply a kiss under the mistletoe, there'd have been no reason to have a big discussion about it not happening again." Adrianna's smile broadened. "Which means it *will* happen again. And I'm betting on sooner, rather than later."

Michelle had barely arrived back at her condo when Kate Dennes called and invited her over.

Apparently Kate was home alone with their eight-year-old daughter and new baby son and desperate for some girl talk. Joel had gotten called into work because of a problem at a job site. When he returned he was having some guys over to play basketball.

"I'd love to see you, Kate, but I was gone most of yesterday and last night." Michelle glanced at Sasha, who stood whining by the door, nudging a leash hanging from a coat hook. "I hate to leave Sasha alone again."

Michelle could have seen if Finley was interested in babysitting Sasha this afternoon, but when she'd gotten home from Hill of Beans, she'd noticed that the condo next door was dark. Apparently Finley and Gabe had gone somewhere for the afternoon.

"Bring Sasha with you," Kate urged. "Chloe would love to read to her before she leaves for her sleepover."

Chloe was a spunky girl and the spitting image

of her beautiful mother. Kate's daughter had met Sasha once before and absolutely adored her.

"Read to her?" Michelle asked. Surely Kate remembered that Sasha was a *dog,* not a small child.

"Apparently they have a westie in their classroom and it's a big deal to read to it," Kate continued. "She's been begging for a puppy."

"Did the argument work?" Michelle remembered how she and her sister had once begged for a dog with good results. "Has the Dennes family welcomed another new member?"

"Not yet. We told Chloe that once Sam starts sleeping through the night, we'll consider it. There's no way I can manage a new baby and a puppy at the same time."

"How is Sam?" Michelle had delivered the nine-pound six ounce boy in an emergency C-section last month.

"Wonderful." Kate expelled a happy sigh. "We're head-over-heels in love with the little guy."

A whisper of melancholy settled around Michelle's shoulders. When she'd been in her twenties she'd thought that by now she'd have a husband and a couple of children like Kate. But here she was, thirty-three and not a boyfriend in sight.

"Please say you'll come over, Michelle. It'll be fun."

"Who all is going to be there?"

"Oh, you mean for the basketball scrimmage?" Kate's tone took on a teasing lilt. "Is there someone special you're hoping to see?"

A vision of Gabe's face flashed before her. "Not really. I was just curious."

"Tripp and David, for sure. Maybe Ryan. I think Betsy was going to some function at the church." Kate paused. "Come for a little bit. You don't have to stay long if you don't want to."

Michelle reminded herself that friends were a blessing that she shouldn't take for granted. Besides, if she didn't go, what was she going to do all afternoon? Mope around and stare wistfully at the town house next door? "I'll grab something to eat and then be right over."

"Don't worry about food. I'm throwing together some sandwiches and other stuff for the guys so there'll be plenty to eat."

"What can I bring?"

"Just yourself and Sasha," Kate said promptly.

"How about snickerdoodle cookies? I baked a batch Friday and if they stay here, I'll eat them all."

"In that case—" Kate laughed "—by all means, bring them. I guarantee you'll be the hit of the party."

The "party" consisted of five hunky men in shorts and T-shirts, a large expanse of concrete and a basketball hoop. Michelle saw several men playing in the back when she drove into the large home's circular drive.

For an afternoon of girl talk and iced tea, Michelle had dressed casually in khaki shorts and a bright blue T. Sasha looked especially festive with a red gingham bandanna looped around her neck.

Chloe bent down when Sasha stepped into the foyer, easing her arms around the dog and burying her head in the golden fur. "Hello, sweet Sasha. Do you want to come with me to my room? It's quiet there and I have tons of books."

Sasha's tail swished slowly from side to side.

Chloe looked up at Michelle. "Is that okay?"

"Fine with me. If your mom approves, that is."

"Why don't you take her into Daddy's office instead?" Kate suggested. "That way if Sasha barks, she won't wake Sam."

"'Kay." Chloe grabbed the dog's collar and the two hurried off.

"How's Sam sleeping?" Michelle asked.

"Great during the day." Kate forced a tired smile. "Not so good at night."

Michelle placed a hand on Kate's arm. "How are you doing?"

"I'm hanging in there." Kate glanced at the

French doors leading outside. "But I'm not quite ready for hoops."

Michelle tilted her head.

Kate laughed. "The guys desperately want another player, but I told them I'm not up to strenuous activity. Not yet, anyway."

"Good call." Michelle winked. "Your doctor wouldn't like it if you opened up those stitches."

The two women walked to the back of the house where five men were in the middle of a game. Beside the court, a patio table held a glass pitcher of tea, two glasses filled with ice and a baby monitor.

Michelle surveyed the court with an experienced eye. Ryan Harcourt, Betsy's husband, had a pretty good jump shot. Tripp lifted a hand in greeting, then swore when David Wahl dribbled around him and tipped the ball through the rim.

Travis Fisher high-fived his best friend while Nick tried to gather up some enthusiasm for his team who'd fallen behind.

"Michelle can be on our team," Tripp called out as she and Kate stopped at the edge of the court.

"Do you want to play?" Nick asked. "If you do, we could sure use you."

"There are five players and that doesn't divide evenly," Kate said in a low tone.

"It doesn't matter if you're good or not." Tripp grabbed the rebound and jogged over.

"I've played a little ball in my time," Michelle said modestly.

"Great," Tripp said, apparently taking the comment as assent.

"I didn't say that I'd do it." Michelle gestured to her friend. "I'm here to chat with Kate."

"She doesn't mind." Tripp slanted a sideways glance at the hostess.

"I'd love to see you…surprise these guys." A twinkle flashed for a second in Kate's eyes, then disappeared.

Michelle suddenly remembered a conversation she'd had with Kate about their respective college days.

"If you want to play, that is." Kate lowered her voice. "I don't want you railroaded into anything."

A familiar adrenaline surge shot through Michelle. "I'd love to play. For a little while."

"We have another player," Tripp announced in a loud voice.

Before Michelle had a chance to step onto the court, one of the cell phones lying on the patio table began to vibrate while emitting a tinny version of the *Jaws* theme.

Kate held it up and glanced around. "Whose phone?"

Travis came trotting over. "Mine."

He took it from her hand, asked a few questions, then clicked it off. "Baby on the way," the obstetrician said. "It's her fourth, so it should come quick."

"Now we're off balanced again," Ryan pointed out.

"Not necessarily." Michelle shoved aside her disappointment and reminded herself she was here to see Kate anyway. "I'm more than happy to sit out."

"Where's Fisher hurrying off to?"

Michelle recognized Gabe's voice immediately. At first she thought Kate might have set her up, until she saw the look of surprise on her friend's face. Apparently Kate hadn't been expecting Gabe either.

"We were kicking his ass and the big baby took his toys and went home," Tripp quickly answered.

"Travis got a call from the hospital. One of his patients is ready to deliver," Michelle clarified, shooting Tripp a look of reproach.

Tripp grinned. "I like my version better."

"Where's Joel?" Kate glanced around Gabe as if hoping her husband would magically appear.

"He went up to check on the baby and see what Chloe was doing."

"She's reading to Sasha," Michelle informed him. She felt, rather than saw, the curiosity in Gabe's gaze.

"I didn't realize you were going to be here," he said.

"Last-minute invitation." Michelle kept her tone light. "Kate can be very persuasive."

"You're preaching to the choir, sister," Joel said with a booming laugh, bending over to give his wife a noisy kiss.

"So is the game off because Fisher left?" Gabe asked, looking magnificent even in dusty jeans and faded T-shirt.

"Naw." Tripp crooked an arm around Michelle's neck. "We've got Kerns."

"Okay, so it's Gabe, David and Ryan against Tripp, Michelle and Nick," Joel announced. "I'll ref."

"Can you review the rules?" While Michelle hadn't played a lot of pickup basketball, she'd played her share. The only consistency was there was no consistency. Rules were fluid and what constituted a foul in one situation didn't in another.

Joel rattled off the basics. The most important was the first team to score seven baskets won.

Michelle knew that pickup games tended to get pretty physical, but she had the feeling the guys would go easy on her which played to her team's advantage. "I take it we're playing with 'no blood, no foul' rules?"

"Don't worry." Tripp settled a hand on her shoulder. "I've got your back, babe."

It was a sweet sentiment. But totally unnecessary...as they would all soon discover.

## Chapter Seven

When Gabe realized Joel was going to let a *woman* play, he couldn't believe it. He'd played a lot of pickup games when he lived in Philadelphia. The one thing all those games had in common was that they were extremely physical.

More than once he'd gone home bleeding. Now Michelle was going to play against him? It didn't make sense, but it wasn't his house or his rules.

She'd taken the ball from Tripp and stood bouncing it, "to get the feel of the ball" she'd said. From the way she was handling it, she'd played a few hoops in her time.

But shooting baskets in a boyfriend's driveway was far different from playing with guys. He wasn't sure why she was doing this when she could be enjoying a glass of iced tea with her friend.

"Are you sure this is a good idea?" he asked Joel in a low tone.

Joel shrugged. "She wants to play."

"Your daughter might want to play, too. That doesn't mean it'd be a good idea." Gabe wasn't sure why he was pushing the issue. After all, it wasn't as if he was Michelle's boyfriend and had to stand up for her.

No, he was definitely not her boyfriend. Far from it.

"You in?" Joel asked.

"I'm in." If any of these guys played rough with her, they were going to answer to him. But as the game progressed, he had the feeling the only one being played was him. When Michelle crowded him, he didn't crowd back…which led to her slipping around him and making the basket.

It wasn't long until he was forced to concede that Michelle wasn't taking up space on the court, she was *good*. She must have played a lot of "horse" in the driveway with her father or with a boyfriend she wanted to impress.

Still, the guys were no slouches either and it was a battle up and down the court. On the last play of the first game, she was driving in for a basket and this time Gabe held his ground, thinking she'd retreat.

She slammed into his chest. Hard. Before he could grab her she fell to the concrete. Gabe's heart rose to his throat. The apology was forming on his lips when she got up and dusted herself off.

"Foul," she called out, pointing to the knee that was bleeding.

He could see she'd also skinned the palm of one hand but it didn't seem to affect her. Or her performance. Her team won not only that game but the second as well.

"I'm ready for some food," Joel said when the second game ended. "How 'bout you guys?"

Michelle pressed the ball against Gabe's chest. "Good game, Davis."

She sauntered over to Kate and they went in the house together to get the food. Gabe hoped Kate would help her clean up her leg and hand while she was in there.

When Michelle came out carrying a platter of sandwiches there was a fresh bandage on her leg and her palm.

Joel wheeled out a cooler filled with beer and soda.

Gabe expected the guys to stay and eat, but everyone except Tripp grabbed a sandwich and a soda and left. Of course all those men had families at home. Finley was spending the day with her new BFF Addie Delacourt, so there wasn't any reason for Gabe to rush off.

While Gabe didn't like to read too much into

situations he wondered if Joel and Kate were doing some matchmaking again. Perhaps that's why Tripp was here. Had Joel and Kate decided the hospital administrator was a good match for Michelle?

Their machinations didn't matter to Gabe. It's just that Michelle seemed very busy right now. For her to start a relationship with Tripp couldn't be good timing.

"This is my kind of party," Kate said happily. "Sandwiches and chips on disposable plates."

"You know, before I start eating I should check on Sasha—" Michelle started to rise.

Kate waved her back down. "She's sleeping. Or she was a few minutes ago when Chloe left."

"Sarabeth's parents know we're picking her up at ten in the morning?" Joel asked his wife.

Kate nodded.

"Not to change the subject, but you've got some serious basketball skills," Joel said to Michelle. "You've played some ball."

"Actually that's what got me through college."

Michelle couldn't keep the pride from her voice. "I played for the University of Wisconsin. Got a full-ride athletic scholarship."

"The perfect trifecta." Tripp directed a warm smile in her direction. "Athletic, smart *and* beautiful."

Gabe's blood began to boil. He didn't like the way Tripp was looking at Michelle. What happened to him and Adrianna? Before Gabe got even more stirred up, he pulled himself up short. Who Michelle dated was none of his business.

Tripp appeared to have no qualms about being with Adrianna last night and making a move on Michelle this afternoon. In fact, he now stood behind her chair giving her a neck and shoulder massage.

From her light moans, she was enjoying it.

Gabe knew he'd been without a woman too long when those breathless little moans and the sight of her neck arching back made his jeans feel tight.

He shifted in his seat and chomped a big bite out

of his sandwich, washing it down with a cool gulp of beer. Because of their matchmaking schemes, being involved with this group of people hadn't been easy. But it appeared they'd found a new man for Michelle, so he was off the hook.

Of course that didn't change the fact that he was Michelle's next-door neighbor. Which meant her welfare was still his concern.

Finley leaned back in the oversize round chair in Addie's bedroom and expelled a happy sigh. Everything about this day had been fun beginning with Lexi, Addie's mom, showing them how to make cream puffs. Then she'd supervised while Finley and Addie had made them on their own. Once they'd finished, Lexi had announced Finley had a natural talent for cooking. As long as Lexi didn't blab that to her dad, Finley figured she'd be okay. The last thing she needed was for her father to think she should do even more of the cooking. Right now they split the duty fifty-fifty.

After an okay dinner of food Finley couldn't

identify, she and Addie had gone upstairs. While they listened to music, her friend pulled out photo albums and scrapbooks. There had been tons of pictures of Addie and her mom, but none of her father. Finley figured he'd been the one taking the pictures.

Finley picked up a photo that hadn't yet made it into a scrapbook.

"Who's this guy?" The older man—he looked about her dad's age—had his arm around Addie, which meant he was probably an uncle or something.

Addie sat cross-legged on the bed. A few strands of hair had slipped from her ponytail and now hung loose to her shoulders. She gazed at the picture for several seconds. A tiny smile lifted the corners of her lips. "That's my father."

Finley took a longer look at the photo. No way was this Addie's father. She'd seen her friend's dad downstairs less than a half hour ago. Even if he'd dyed his hair blond for a prank, the nose and shape of his face was all wrong. "No, really, who is he?"

Addie took the picture from her hand and pointed to the man with a hot pink-tipped fingernail. "My father."

"Then who's the guy downstairs?"

"Nick is my stepdad," Addie announced in a matter-of-fact tone.

"No way."

"Way."

"You didn't tell me your mom was married before."

"She wasn't." Addie's cheeks took on a pinkish tinge. "They never got married."

"How long ago did they split?"

"Before I was born." Addie dropped her gaze. "He didn't want kids."

Even though her friend's tone was light, Finley knew there had to be some pissed-off feelings lurking beneath. "We have that in common."

Addie frowned. "What do you mean?"

"My mom didn't want me either." Finley's tone sounded flat even to her ears. "Still doesn't."

She explained how her mother had stuck around for a couple months, then decided having fun in college was more important than being a mom. Of course, that wasn't how her father told it, but Finley was smart enough to read between the lines.

"My dad gave my mom a choice, him or me." Addie's eyes were solemn. "She chose me."

"She told you that?" Finley had concluded it was some sort of parent code that they kept such stuff from their kids. But if Lexi had told Addie the truth...

"No," Addie said, "I overheard her telling one of her friends."

Finley looked at the picture again. Addie's dad had his arm around her and they were both smiling. "If he was my dad, I think I'd hate him."

Actually there was no "think" about it. Finley hated her mom for leaving her.

"I kinda hated him once." Addie's eyes took on a faraway look. "I don't anymore."

"Why not?"

"I talked to my parents and to a counselor. They helped me figure everything out. Bottom line was my dad was sorry for being stupid back then. I've done stupid things, too. How could I not forgive him?"

"I don't know if I could…forgive him, I mean."

Addie cocked her head. "Do you hate your mother?"

"I don't think about her." It was mostly true. Except on Mother's Day—when the world seemed to go crazy for moms—and on her birthday, when Finley couldn't help wondering if this would be the year her mother would send her a card.

"Do you think your dad will ever get married?"

Finley lifted a shoulder in a slight shrug as if it didn't matter one way or the other. The truth was, it scared the spit out of her.

"Drew doesn't like it that I call Nick my dad, but I don't care," Addie said. "I tell him I'm lucky because I have two dads."

A sigh slipped past Finley's lips. Addie had

two fathers and she didn't even have *one* mother. "You're very lucky."

"If your dad married your neighbor," Addie declared, as if she could read Finley's mind, "you'd have a mother."

"Are you talking about Michelle?"

"No, I'm talking about Mrs. McGregor, the crazy old woman on the other side of you." Addie rolled her eyes. "My dad said he saw your father and Michelle this afternoon playing basketball at Chloe's house. And didn't they go to Mr. and Mrs. Fisher's party together?"

Finley blinked. "He—he says they're just friends."

Addie stared at her for a long moment, then uncrossed her legs and swung them off the side of the bed. "Don't you want them to get together? I thought you liked her."

"She seems nice," Finley said cautiously. "I don't know her that well."

"That's smart."

"What is?"

"Wanting to make sure she's worthy of your dad."

Finley didn't remember saying anything about being concerned about Michelle not being worthy. Still, Addie had a point. "How would I know if she is or not?"

"A series of tests." Addie's lips curved up. "Designed to bring out the worst in her."

Finley's first reaction was to tell Addie she was crazy, but she stopped herself. In the few short weeks since she'd met Addie, she'd discovered that her new friend was super-smart. "Why would we do that?"

"Because if there's even a chance she could end up being your stepmother, you need to know what you're up against."

"I might be late getting home," Gabe told his daughter the next morning. "The chamber of commerce committee I was assigned to decided to meet after work instead of over lunch."

"I'll make myself a sandwich." Finley jumped

on the news. "Because it's hard to know when you'll be home."

Gabe hid a smile. He knew part of his daughter's easy acquiescence had to do with the fact that it was her night to cook. "I'm not sure if we'll stop somewhere for a quick dinner or not, but I'll call once I know how long I'll be."

Finley picked up her cereal bowl and took it to the sink. "Tell me again who's on the committee."

Her back was to him, so Gabe couldn't see his daughter's face. It was, he told himself, a natural question. Then why did he feel as if there was something more going on?

"Michelle, Adrianna, Tripp and me." Gabe wondered if Tripp would give Michelle a ride. Last night when he'd left the Denneses' home, she and Tripp had been talking by her car.

Turning on the water, Finley rinsed out the bowl. "Will you and Michelle be driving together?"

"Why do you ask?"

"You live next door to each other," she said in

a casual tone that gave nothing away. "With the price of gas it only makes sense."

"I don't think so," Gabe said. "Although she may ride with Tripp."

Finley turned around, the bowl dripping in her hand. "Why would she ride with him?"

Gabe pushed aside his plate, no longer hungry. "I think they may be dating."

"Really?"

There was a look in Finley's eyes that Gabe couldn't quite identify.

"Tripp is a nice guy. They'd make a good couple." He wondered who he was trying to convince.

"You okay with that?"

Gabe gave a laugh, even though he wasn't feeling particularly lighthearted at the moment. "Why wouldn't I be?"

"I thought you liked her."

"Michelle is a nice woman. And a good neighbor," Gabe told his daughter. "But I meant what I told Grandma and Grandpa. This first year in

Jackson Hole I'm focusing on my job and on you."

"So if Michelle wants Tripp—"

"She can date whomever she wants. It's okay with me," Gabe spoke decisively, hoping if he said the words aloud and with great gusto, he'd believe them.

## Chapter Eight

The committee had agreed to meet at the site being considered for the veterans memorial garden. Gabe had been working in the mountains, so the other three members were already there by the time he arrived.

"Sorry I'm late." He slammed his truck door and hurried across the grassy lot. "A client unexpectedly stopped by and threw everything behind."

"I had two lovely ladies to keep me company." Tripp smiled, gesturing to Michelle and Adrianna. "I didn't even notice you weren't here."

Gabe still wore his boots, jeans and work shirt, while Michelle looked especially nice in a red dress that wrapped itself around her curves. Simple, yet enticing, it sent his thoughts in a direction he didn't want to go. Even though she was wearing flat shoes today, his eyes couldn't help but be drawn to her legs. Shapely and long enough to wrap around a man...

"What do you think?" Tripp asked.

Gabe jerked his gaze upward and saw a twinkle in Tripp's eyes.

"I think having a groundbreaking ceremony is a good idea," Michelle saved him by answering.

"It would be a good way to make the community aware of the project." Adrianna took a step back and looked over the grassy plain as if visualizing the scene.

"We could have the mayor and all the city officials here for the ground breaking and then have a celebration at a bar or a restaurant afterward." Gabe thought for a moment. "At the celebration we could put up the architect's drawing of the finished memorial—"

"—and have a place for people to sign up to sponsor a brick," Michelle added, her voice quivering with excitement.

"Bricks?" Adrianna asked. "I don't remember a discussion about bricks."

"According to this drawing—" Michelle held up a sheet of paper and pointed "—there will be a row of bricks on both sides of the walkway leading to the memorial. I assumed we'd want the public to be able to buy those bricks in honor of a veteran. They could have them inscribed with the name of the service member."

"You're a genius." Tripp planted a noisy kiss on her cheek. "Not only would it add to the community buy-in, but the extra money could also be used if the construction costs run over."

He left his arm looped around Michelle's shoulder, but a moment later she took a step away, dislodging it.

Adrianna stilled at Gabe's side, the wind fluttering the papers she held in her hand.

"Let's adjourn and continue this discussion at the new wine bar on Broadway," Tripp suggested. "A glass of pinot noir with some pad thai sounds good."

"Is Finley home tonight?" Michelle pulled out her cell phone. "She took Sasha out at noon, but that was almost six hours ago. I wonder if she'd be interested in walking her again?"

Gabe recalled the pride on his daughter's face when she'd added up all the money she'd earned so far this summer. "I can't speak for her, but I'm sure she'll be happy to help. As far as I know, the only thing on her agenda for the evening was to watch a movie and talk to Addie."

"That's why I don't have any pets," Tripp announced. "Dogs are a lot of work."

"I agree." Adrianna met his gaze and the two shared a smile.

"You don't know what you're missing," Michelle retorted as she pulled out her phone and called Finley. As Gabe had anticipated, his daughter immediately agreed. Because Michelle had given her a key when she'd begun watching Sasha, nothing more needed to be done.

While Michelle had been speaking with Finley, Adrianna and Tripp had been raving over items on the wine bar's menu such as pad thai, which Gabe learned contained tofu. Ugh. And braised pork belly. Not a hamburger in sight.

"I've an idea." Gabe focused on Tripp. "You check out the wine bar. I'm going to head over to The Coffee Pot."

Adrianna's brows pulled together and confusion blanketed her face. "Surely you're not seriously thinking of having the celebration there?"

"No," Gabe said honestly. "I'm thinking how much I want a hamburger. Or perhaps a hunk of meatloaf with scalloped potatoes. Tofu just won't cut it tonight."

He shifted his gaze to Michelle. "But it's no fun eating alone."

The beautiful blonde doctor slanted a quick

sideways glance at Adrianna and Tripp. "I'm in the mood for a hamburger, too."

Almost immediately Adrianna turned to Tripp. "If you'd prefer to go with Gabe and Michelle I can check out the wine bar myself."

Tripp's hesitation confused Gabe. Was it Adrianna? Was the hospital administrator concerned she might think this was a date? Or did he want to spend the evening with Michelle?

A possessive feeling gripped Gabe at the thought. But something in Tripp's eyes when he looked at Adrianna told him he had nothing to worry about. If he was worried. Which he wasn't. Not at all.

"I'll check out the wine bar with you. We can see if it has enough space for a postgroundbreaking celebration while enjoying some terrific food." Tripp's gaze shifted to Gabe and Michelle. "You two can discuss the concept of selling bricks in honor of veterans. That way, when we get back together for our next meeting, we'll have moved ahead."

"No worries." Gabe spoke to Tripp as he shot Michelle a wink. "We'll get 'er done."

Because he and Michelle had both driven to the proposed site, they agreed to meet at the café. On the way downtown, Gabe found himself wondering was it the hamburger he wanted? Or Michelle?

By the time Michelle parked her car and walked to The Coffee Pot she'd had plenty of time to wonder where she'd left her head. Going out to dinner with Gabe? Alone? Whatever had she been thinking?

*But I want a burger,* she told herself, *not Asian cuisine.*

Besides, it was obvious—to her at least—that Adrianna would kill for some alone time with Tripp. And that's exactly what Michelle had given her. In exchange she was getting a nice juicy hamburger and…Gabe.

Speak of the devil.

Michelle's heart gave a little flutter. Dressed

casually in jeans and boots, Gabe stood in front of the café, obviously waiting for her. As she drew close, she grudgingly admitted she found his rugged outdoorsy look appealing. "You could have gone inside."

"If I had, who'd have done this?" A tanned arm sprinkled with a dusting of dark hair reached around her to pull open the door. He gestured for her to enter ahead of him.

There was no reason for her to pause in the doorway where mere inches separated them. No reason except to savor the scent of soap, sawdust and something else she couldn't identify. As she moved past him, Michelle felt the gentle brush of his hand on her back. A shiver traveled up her spine.

All through dinner there was something in the air. A curious intensity that made the meatloaf melt in her mouth and the potatoes taste as if they'd been seasoned by a cordon bleu-trained chef.

By the time dessert was on the table, they'd

covered a lot of ground, including wrapping up the discussion on the memorial bricks. Michelle would have been hard pressed to recall everything they discussed. All she knew was the conversation flowed as easily as the coffee.

She reflected on all the interesting facts she'd learned about her dinner partner. Such as, from the time he was a little boy, Gabe had liked to build things.

"Is that how you ended up in home building?" Michelle forked off a piece of pie, not hungry but not yet ready for the evening to end.

"After Finley was born I worked construction. I discovered I liked using my hands as well as my mind." A smile lifted his lips. "By the time she was in school, I was able to start college. It took me a while, but last year I obtained a degree in construction engineering."

"That's a difficult course of study." Michelle felt his eyes follow the cherries and crust to her lips. Her mouth began to tingle and she forced the bite past the sudden tightness in her throat with a sip of coffee.

"It's hard." His eyes never left hers.

Michelle's heart picked up speed. She licked her suddenly dry lips and considered the wisdom of continuing this topic. Reluctantly she changed the subject. "What made you decide to settle in Jackson Hole?"

The slight lift to his lips told her she hadn't fooled anyone, least of all him.

"I wanted a good place to raise Finley and a job that wouldn't consume my life." He spread his hands on the table and leaned forward. "Don't get me wrong, I'm willing to work hard, but I believe in the importance of a balanced life."

When Michelle had married Ed, a sense of balance between career and home was something she'd wanted, too. Since her divorce, maintaining that equilibrium had become increasingly more difficult. Lately her life had been ninety percent medicine, eight percent Sasha and two percent everything else.

"I'm surprised you haven't married again," she heard Gabe say. "You're smart, beautiful and you have one heckuva jump shot."

Michelle pulled her thoughts back to the present. "I guess I've never found a man who could tempt me to walk down that aisle again." A smile twisted her lips, although she found no humor in the admission. "Once bitten, twice shy. You know."

"What are your deal breakers?"

She cocked her head.

"What makes you cross a guy off the possibility list?"

"If I had any 'deal breakers'—" she lifted her fingers and did the quotes in the air "—what makes you think I'd tell you?"

"Why not?" His amber eyes were surprisingly serious. "We've decided it's best if you and I are simply neighbors. But let's say I have a guy in mind for you. How do I know if he'd be suitable?"

Even though what Gabe was saying made sense, having him matchmake for her felt wrong on so many levels. Suddenly irritated, Michelle shoved a strand of hair back from her face. "I suppose you have someone in mind?"

Gabe paused as if weighing the consequences of his words. "Tripp Randall?"

Even before the entire name had left his lips, Michelle began shaking her head.

"Why not?"

Although Tripp was a nice guy, he belonged with Adrianna, even if right now he refused to see it. Besides, she didn't find his sculpted features and mop of blond hair sexy. "I prefer men with dark hair."

Michelle didn't realize she'd spoken the words aloud until Gabe smiled.

The glint in Gabe's eyes drew heat to the surface of her skin. "I have dark hair."

Michelle cleared her throat. "You're also my neighbor."

"Right." He pushed his empty plate off to the side. "Now about those deal breakers…"

Michelle wished she could be honest. But if

she told him having a teenage child was a deal breaker, he'd argue. Tell her not all kids are the same. Insist there were many kids out there—like his daughter—who were terrific. All possibly valid statements.

But each time Michelle was tempted to get sucked in by such logic, she remembered Ed's daughters and how nice they'd seemed...at first. She couldn't allow herself to care for Finley or to start really liking her, only to discover the teenager was an enemy in disguise.

"C'mon, Michi," he said in a low, teasing tone that somehow managed to sound seductive.

She gave her hormones a good hard shake and him a dark glance. "My name is Michelle."

Okay, so maybe she sounded a tad cross, but he wasn't making this easy. And when he took her hand, lightly caressing her palm with his thumb, she realized he had no intention of letting up until he got what he wanted.

"*Michelle,* give me something to work with here."

"If he likes clothes more than I do," she blurted out, snatching back her hand.

"What?"

"If a guy likes clothes more than I do, it's a deal breaker."

For a second Gabe appeared thrown off guard. He glanced down at his T-shirt and jeans. His lips twitched. "What else?"

"That's it for tonight."

A slow grin spread across his face. "I can't believe you're shutting me off."

"Believe it."

"You know what this means?" He picked up her hand once again, but this time resisted her attempts to pull away.

The touch of his fingers caused a ripple of sensation to run up her arm. Michelle drew air slowly into her lungs. "No. Tell me. What does it mean?"

"We're going to have to do this again." A devilish gleam filled his eyes. "If I get only one deal breaker at a time, you and I are going to have to eat a whole lot of meals together before I have enough information to play matchmaker."

She thought about telling him she hadn't asked him to play matchmaker, didn't want him to play matchmaker, but she was afraid if she was that blunt, the banter would stop. She'd enjoyed laughing and talking with him over meatloaf, scalloped potatoes and cherry pie. She wouldn't even mind having dinner with him again. Just as friends, of course.

Despite his protests, when the bill came, Michelle insisted on paying for her own dinner. After all, she reminded him, this wasn't a date.

"Where did you park?" He cupped her elbow as they made their way through the crowded café to the outside sidewalk.

Michelle pointed to the right in a vague gesture. "A couple blocks that way. How about you?"

"Right there."

His red truck sat parked almost directly in front of the café. She wasn't sure how she'd missed it.

"Well." She held out her hand. "Good night."

Gabe responded with a long stare and ignored her outstretched hand. "I'm not letting you walk to your car alone."

"It's two blocks away, three at the most." Michelle gave a little laugh. "This is Jackson Hole, not Philly. I'll be perfectly safe."

"I'm walking with you." He took her arm and his eyes took on an impish gleam. "Maybe I'll be lucky and you'll share another deal breaker on the way."

Michelle drove into her garage. She was ready to lower the door when she realized she owed Finley for the extra time she'd spent with Sasha.

While payment could easily wait until tomorrow, she knew how much the girl looked forward to the money. She was still debating whether to go over and ring the bell when Gabe pulled into his driveway. He parked the truck in the garage, then immediately came out to greet her.

"Decided to share another deal breaker with me?" he said by way of greeting.

"Shut up." She held out several bills.

Gabe lifted a brow, looking amused. "You're paying me to shut up?"

"Of course not." Michelle felt herself melting under the glow of his boyish grin. "This is for Finley. It's her payment for watching Sasha this evening."

"In that case…"

He reached out. She expected him to pluck the money from her fingers. Instead, his hand closed over hers and he tugged her close.

"What are you doing?" she stammered.

A glint entered his eyes. "Thanking you properly for a very pleasant evening."

The air had turned chilly, but when Gabe pulled her tight against his body, heat flowed through Michelle's veins like an awakened river.

*He's going to kiss me. He's going to kiss me. He's going to kiss me.*

There was time for her to pull back. To walk inside. To go to bed. Alone.

His gaze searched hers, dark and intense.

"Well, if you're going to say thank you, go ahead and do it, I mean, *say* it."

His lips curved up. Without another word, his mouth closed over hers.

Finley had been on the phone with Addie for about twenty minutes when she heard Michelle's garage door go up.

"I don't think there's anything between them," she told Addie.

"Really? You don't think we need to test her?"

Finley didn't know why Addie even bothered to ask, because before she had a chance to reply, Addie went on to give all the reasons she thought they should still move forward with their plan.

When Finley had been at Addie's yesterday they'd come up a whole list of possible "tests" designed to bring out Michelle's true self. But now that she'd had more time to think about it, Finley decided they'd overreacted. Michelle and her dad had never even been on a date. Even tonight had been purely business.

Trying to think of a good response, Finley idly glanced outside where her dad and Michelle stood talking on the driveway. Was it only her imagination or were they now standing closer together? Finley narrowed her gaze, then gasped as her dad pulled Michelle to him. When he kissed their neighbor, a tiny squeak slipped past her lips.

"What is it?" she heard her friend say. "Is something wrong?"

"My dad and Michelle just got home from their meeting and he's—" Finley swallowed hard "—kissing her."

"A friendly peck on the cheek? Or a *Jersey Shore* kind of kiss?"

"Yuck." With her stomach churning, Finley turned away from the window. "I can't watch anymore."

*"Jersey Shore,"* she heard Addie murmur.

Finley pressed her lips together. "I've reconsidered."

"You're going to take another look?"

"Absolutely not." Finley drew a deep breath,

keeping her eyes away from the window. She knew her dad had probably kissed other women, but thankfully she'd never had to witness such grossness before. "I'm talking about the tests. We need to find out what Michelle is really like... and soon."

## Chapter Nine

When Gabe thought about the kiss he and Michelle had shared, he reluctantly admitted there was a thousand other ways he could have thanked her for a nice evening. But he didn't regret his action. There'd been a spark between them that was hard to resist.

Still, he was convinced that Michelle would tell him he needed to keep his hands—and his mouth—to himself. But days passed and that never happened.

Yet, he noticed a subtle shift in their relationship after that night. It wasn't anything big, but rather a series of small things: a casual call now and then, an offer to pick up stuff at the store, bringing a plate of cookies over one night. By all indications, their friendship had deepened.

Gabe didn't spend a lot of time analyzing the situation or even thinking about it. He was too busy. The construction season was in full swing and Stone Craft Builders was on target to have its best year ever.

Two weeks later he was at a job site in the mountains when his phone buzzed indicating a new text message. He pulled it from his pocket and glanced at the screen.

"Is that the lumberyard?" Joel took off his hat and wiped the sweat from his brow.

They'd been at the job site of a new home in the mountains since early that morning. Although the pine trees provided some relief from the sun, at eleven-fifteen it was already unseasonably warm.

A smile lifted Gabe's lips and he held up the phone so Joel could see the readout.

The text from Michelle was simple and to the point: *Lunch?*

Joel grinned. "I thought at the party there was something going on between you and our star basketball player."

"There's not," Gabe protested but without much force. "We're just neighbors."

Joel rubbed his chin. "You know, I can't recall the last time I texted one of my neighbors about having lunch."

"Michelle and I like the same kinds of food." Gabe went on to tell his boss about the meat-loaf dinner they'd shared a couple weeks earlier at The Coffee Pot. "It seems like most women nowadays are into sushi and tofu. But Michelle is a real meat-and-potatoes kind of gal."

"I'm sure her love of meatloaf is the attraction," Joel murmured.

"What?" Gabe cocked his head. The framers had been yelling to each other and he hadn't been able to hear clearly.

"I said, have lunch with her," Joel replied, this

time in a loud booming voice. "While you're in town you can pick up those extra supplies the lumberyard forgot to deliver."

Even though Gabe had been ready to text his regrets, having lunch with Michelle was definitely a step up from the sandwich and apple he'd brought for lunch.

"Go now," Joel urged. "It's not good to keep a neighbor waiting."

Something about the way Joel emphasized "neighbor" made Gabe pause. "There's nothing going on between me and Michelle."

"I understand. You simply like the same kind of food," Joel reminded him, the look in his eyes turning into a twinkle.

Gabe lifted his hands, one still holding the phone. "I'm serious."

"I believe you." Joel shifted his gaze down to his tool belt and picked up a hammer, suddenly all business. "I've got everything under control here, so there's no need to rush back."

Gabe stood there for a second before deciding there was no reason to say more. He'd just reached the door to his truck when he heard Joel call his name. He turned back.

"Enjoy the meatloaf," his boss called out, a smirk on his lips.

"I can't believe we wasted an afternoon coming up with those tests and haven't done a single one," Addie grumbled.

A shopping bag swung from each girl's hand. Lexi had dropped them off in downtown Jackson this morning and would pick them up after lunch.

"Her kiss must have turned off my dad." Finley smiled at the thought. "I know he hasn't kissed her again."

Addie paused in front of a shoe store window, her eyes taking on a gleam as she studied a pair of sandals decorated with brightly colored stones.

"How can you be so sure?" Addie asked, pulling her gaze from the shoes.

"All he does lately is work." Finley thought

for a moment. "I bet I see Michelle more than he does."

"So you're still watching Sasha?"

"Every day." Warmth flowed through Finley. She adored Sasha. Taking the golden retriever for a walk was the highlight of her day. And her short talks with Michelle were nice, too. It turned out they shared a common interest in basketball and Sasha. "I can see why Michelle loves her. She's a super-sweet dog."

"That's why that test we came up with where Sasha goes missing is pure genius. Talk about stressing Michelle to the max."

Actually it was Addie who'd come up with the idea. Just the thought of dog-napping Sasha made Finley sick to her stomach.

"We're not doing that unless it's absolutely necessary," Finley said, then promptly changed the subject. She glanced down the street. Because Jackson catered to the tourist trade, the small town had lots of restaurants. "What sounds good for lunch?"

Addie thought for a moment. "How about pizza? Sound good to you?"

Finley nodded and sniffed the air. "I smell pepperoni."

Her friend smirked. "Perfect Pizza is just around the corner."

In a matter of minutes, the girls had reached the restaurant and placed their order at the counter. Finley picked up the table flag and plastic utensils. Addie carried the glasses of soda. The dining room was only about half full, which Finley guessed was fairly typical for a Monday.

"Let's sit in a booth," Addie turned to the left where a series of wooden booths with high backs lined the wall. "It's more private. We can talk about Justin and Zac without anyone overhearing."

Justin and Zac were Justin Bieber and Zac Efron. While their parents might think they were too young to date, that didn't mean they weren't interested in boys. They'd decided a week ago that Justin would be Addie's out-of-state "boy-friend" while Zac belonged to Finley.

Finley had to admit—but only to herself—that seeing her dad kiss Michelle had made her begin to wonder what it would be like to kiss Zac....

"Ohmigod," Addie squeaked.

Finley looked up. Her heart plummeted to the tips of her royal blue ballet flats.

"Hi, honey." Her dad slipped from the booth where he'd been sitting with Michelle. He rocked back on his bootheels. "What a surprise. I didn't expect to see you here."

Finley lifted her chin, her jaw so tightly clenched that it ached. Hurt and a sense of betrayal welled inside her. "I thought you were at work."

"I was, I mean, I am. I came into Jackson to have lunch with Michelle."

Her dad seemed to stumble over the words, which told Finley he had something to hide.

"I made your lunch last night," Finley reminded him. She'd gone to a lot of work making that ham-

and-cheese sandwich. And she'd even washed the apple—and wrapped it in a paper towel—before she'd dropped it into the brown sack. She couldn't help wondering how many other lunches he'd shared with Michelle that he never bothered to mention.

"Yes, and I'm planning on eating it tomorrow." Her dad's eyes flashed a warning. "Today, I'm enjoying pizza."

"Hi, Finley," Michelle greeted her, then shifted her gaze to Addie and smiled. "Is your mom with you?"

Addie shook her head. "She's working this morning."

"Mrs. Delacourt dropped us off so we could do some shopping," Finley explained. "She's picking us up during her lunch hour and taking us to my place."

"Why don't you girls join us?" Gabe smiled and gestured to the booth.

"Thank you, but Finley and I—" Addie glanced

at her friend, appearing to have lost her voice midexcuse.

"We don't want to disturb you," Finley continued and her friend nodded.

"Besides, we can't stay long," Addie added. "My mom will be at the Antler Arch to pick us up real soon."

"If you're sure…" Gabe said.

"We're sure." Knowing her dad would be upset if she continued to ignore Michelle, Finley plastered a smile on her face and shifted her gaze back to the doctor. "Nice to see you again. Enjoy the pizza."

"C'mon, Addie." Finley grabbed her friend's arm, careful not to tip the sodas in her hands. "Let's find a table by the window."

She chose a wooden table with thick sturdy bench seats way across the room from where her dad and Michelle sat. Shortly after their pizza arrived, Finley turned to Addie. "It's time for a test."

Addie's eyes never left her friend's face. "When?"

Finley glanced in the direction of the booths. "I say the sooner the better."


"I'm sorry if this is awkward for you." Michelle waited to speak until the girls were out of earshot. She'd recognized the look in Finley's eyes. His daughter had not been pleased. "I didn't think our having lunch would be such a big deal."

Gabe had resumed his seat across from her. He grabbed another slice of pizza. "It's not."

"Finley didn't seem happy about it."

"She was surprised to see me here. Like I was surprised to see her and Addie."

Michelle forced a bite of pizza past the sudden lump in her throat. Just like Ed, Gabe couldn't see what was right under his nose.

Finley didn't like her. The sharp pain in her heart surprised Michelle. She'd been close to letting down her guard around the girl. Their lively conversations about basketball had felt natural.

"I'm glad you invited me to lunch." Gabe smiled across the table at her. "Made my day."

"We hadn't seen much of each other recently." Michelle kept her tone light and breezy. She decided there was no reason to address her concerns about Gabe having his head in the sand regarding his daughter because they didn't matter. She and Gabe were friends. Nothing more.

Michelle still wasn't sure what had possessed her to text him and ask him to lunch. A momentary bit of craziness, that's for sure.

Until Finley's arrival and sudden coldness toward her, she and Gabe had been having a nice time. He was an interesting guy and fun to be around. With him, she could relax and be herself.

He leaned forward and rested his arms on the table. His amber eyes took on a familiar gleam. "Are you ready to share another deal breaker with me?"

"Nope." Michelle chopped the word. It was beginning to annoy her that he seemed so focused on finding her a man.

"C'mon, Michi. Help me help you."

Michelle used to adore that nickname. But then her former stepdaughter had taken it up and made it almost a slur. She couldn't hear it without thinking of them.

She grasped the edge of the table with both hands and pinned Gabe with her gaze. "*If* and *when* I decide to jump into dating again, I am fully capable of making my own matches. And it's not Michi. My name is *Michelle*."

Gabe just grinned and took another bite of pizza.

Michelle decided the man was incorrigible. "Because you seem so interested in the topic, why don't you tell me *your* deal breakers, Gabe?"

She expected him to hesitate or turn the conversation back to her. Instead he said one word. "Finley."

Michelle's slice of pizza fell from her hand back to the plate. "Beg your pardon?"

"Whoever I date, whoever I consider marrying will need to understand that Finley and I are a package deal." His eyes were clear and direct. "I'll never get serious about any woman who considers my daughter a nuisance. Finley is a great kid. She deserves a stepmom who will love and cherish her just as much as I do."

The raw emotion in Gabe's voice touched a chord in Michelle's heart. She'd known he loved his daughter, but this time she *felt* it. Here was a man with a great capacity for love.

A love that would never be hers. While Michelle liked Finley, she couldn't imagine letting her guard down long enough for the girl into her heart. And from Gabe's impassioned speech, it was apparent that her inability to love his daughter would be the ultimate deal breaker.

"Are you positively triple-dog-dare sure that he can be trusted?" Finley ignored the boy standing next to Addie and held on tight to Sasha's collar, keeping the dog protectively by her side.

"Absolutely." Addie glanced up at the tall geeky

boy with a bad case of acne. "He'll take super-good care of Sasha. Right, Josh?"

Josh nodded and swallowed convulsively, his Adam's apple bobbing up and down in his thin neck. "I'll drive him around with me. Then, at eight o'clock, I'll sneak him into my neighbor's fenced yard. She works at the animal shelter, so once she discovers a strange dog has shown up, that will be the first place she'll call."

"Sasha is a her, not a him." Finley had a bad feeling about this "test," but knowing her dad had been sneaking around behind her back had given her a bad feeling, too.

"Give her to him, Finley," Addie urged, glancing around furtively. "My mom will be here to pick me up any minute. She can't see Josh."

Reluctantly Finley let the boy snap a leash on Sasha's collar and the dog willingly hopped into the cab of the boy's truck. They were out of sight in minutes.

"She'll be okay." Addie squeezed Finley's hand

as they went back inside. "Josh is a huge animal lover. He'll take good care of her."

"How can you be sure?" She liked it that Josh had come the second Addie had called him, but that still didn't mean he could be trusted with Sasha.

"I've known him forever," Addie said. "He's Coraline's nephew."

Her friend said the words as if that should clear away the doubts. Instead Finley felt no more reassured than she had seconds before. "Who?"

"Coraline runs a bed-and-breakfast. My mom used to work for her."

"I thought your mother was a social worker?"

"She is, but before she married Nick, she had two jobs. I call Coraline my Wyoming grandma." Addie smiled. "When we were little, Josh and I used to play together all the time. Now that he's seventeen, I don't see him much."

"If anything happens to Sasha…"

"Nothing will happen to her." A gleam filled

Addie's eyes. "But you will get to see how Michelle reacts under stress."

"Sasha is her baby." That sick feeling filled the pit of Finley's stomach. Michelle loved the golden retriever the way most people loved their kids. "She's going to freak when she realizes she's gone."

"We wouldn't be doing this if it wasn't important." Addie's eyes took on a faraway look. "My mom once dated a guy who seemed nice, but he went ballistic one day when someone did a hit-and-run on his car in a parking lot. He got so angry that my mom and I were afraid he was going to hit *us*. She never saw him again after that night."

Even though Finley didn't think Michelle would ever slug her or her dad, the pretty doctor did seem too nice to be true. And she'd learned that people could be different than they appeared. When it came to women, she couldn't rely on her father's judgment. Take her mother, for example. Her dad had liked her, too.

Look at how that had turned out....

# *Chapter Ten*

Michelle arrived home a little later than she had planned that night. As she pulled into the driveway, she noticed the light on in Gabe's kitchen.

A smile lifted her lips as she pictured him sitting at the table being interrogated by his daughter. It was obvious the girl hadn't been pleased to see her with Gabe.

Michelle wished she could think of a way to tell Finley she didn't need to worry.

As the garage door closed behind her car, Michelle waited for Sasha to welcome her home.

Instead of staccato barks, only silence greeted her. Could Finley have taken her for a walk? Or perhaps Sasha was outside, in the small fenced area off the back deck?

Despite all sorts of logical possibilities Michelle hurried into the house, her heart moving as fast as her feet. "Sasha," she called out. "Mommy's home."

Michelle paused and listened. No toenails clicking on the hardwood floor. No little whines of delight. Only the heavy thumping of her own heart.

By the time she'd searched every room, Michelle's voice had begun to crack and she found it increasingly difficult to breathe. Holding on to the hope that she'd find Sasha safely in the backyard, Michelle stepped outside and called some more. By the time she reached the fence and saw the gate ajar, she was light-headed. She took several deep breaths, telling herself it wasn't as bad as it looked.

Obviously Finley had taken her for a walk. Yes, that had to be it. The girl had noticed Michelle had been running late, had seen Sasha in the backyard and had taken it upon herself to help. Sasha was probably sitting by Gabe's table at this moment begging for scraps.

With shaky hands, Michelle wiped away the tears that had leaked from her lids. She squared her shoulders and headed across the lawn, praying all the way.

The knock at the back door took Gabe by surprise. He and Finley had just finished dinner and he wasn't expecting anyone to stop by.

He glanced at his daughter. Her one-shoulder shrug told him she was equally puzzled.

"I'll see who it is." Gabe pushed back his chair. When he opened the door, he saw Michelle. Twice in one day. This could get to be a habit. A very pleasant one. He smiled. "What a nice surprise."

Before he'd even finished speaking, Michelle was inside, glancing around. "Is she here?"

"Finley is in the other room." For the first time

Gabe noticed the frantic look in her eyes. "Is something wrong?"

"I'm looking for Sasha." Michelle's voice shook with emotion. "Is she over here?"

Finley appeared in the doorway. "What's going on?"

"I'm not sur—"

"Is Sasha here?" Michelle cut him off, her gaze now riveted to Finley.

His daughter shook her head.

"I need to know the last time you saw her. It could be important." Michelle paused and took a deep breath. It was obvious to Gabe that she was trying to hold onto her control. "Sasha is missing."

His daughter's face paled. "I saw her earlier this afternoon when I walked her. She seemed fine."

"What time did you walk her?" Michelle took a step toward Finley.

Finley's eyes widened. "I—I don't know for sure. Probably around two."

Michelle crossed the room in several long

strides to where Finley stood. "Are you the one who left the gate open?"

"I was with Addie all afternoon." Finley's voice quivered and she looked at him.

"You must have left the gate open when you walked her at two," Michelle muttered. "It's after eight now."

Even though Michelle hadn't moved from where she stood, Finley took a step back. "I put her in the house after we walked."

"I always latch the gate," Michelle said, almost to herself. "I double and triple check it to make sure it's latched. It had to be you."

Finley's face blanched as if she'd been slapped.

"Wait a minute." Gabe slid a reassuring arm around Finley's shoulders. "I know you're upset, Michelle, but it sounds like you're blaming Finley for Sasha's disappearance."

Michelle whirled, her eyes wet with unshed tears. "Sasha is missing. Don't you understand?"

"And Finley and I are going to do everything we can to help get her back." He glanced at his daughter who nodded. "But I won't have you blaming Finley for something that isn't her fault. Who knows how the gate got unlatched? Maybe some kid opened it to play with Sasha this afternoon and forgot to close it."

"There are no kids in this area, Gabe." Michelle clasped her trembling hands together. "Only Finley and Mrs. McGregor are home during the day."

"Have you spoken with Mrs. McGregor?" Gabe gentled his tone. "Maybe she saw something."

"Dad." Finley's hand touched his shirt sleeve. "Mrs. McGregor volunteers at the hospital on Monday afternoons."

"Great." Michelle raked her fingers through her hair and closed her eyes. "No witnesses to the crime."

"We don't know there was a crime." Gabe kept his tone soft and low. "If the gate wasn't firmly latched, Sasha could have pushed on it and decided to do some exploring."

Michelle's face crumpled. "I don't know what I'll do if anything happens to her."

Gabe told himself to keep his hands off her, especially with Finley standing there, but he couldn't hold back any longer. He pulled Michelle close. "It will be okay. We'll find her."

"Sasha is all I have," she whispered against his shirtfront.

Tears slipped down her cheeks. Gabe let her cry, stroking the back of her head. He glanced at Finley who appeared rooted where she stood. "Honey, could you please call the animal shelter and see if anyone has reported finding a golden?"

"I didn't leave the gate open," Finley said, not moving a muscle.

"No one is saying you did, Finley."

"She did." Finley pointed to Michelle who'd stepped back from Gabe's arms and stood swiping at her tears. "She tried to blame this all on me."

Great. Now he had two upset females on his hands.

"I'm sorry." Michelle's red-rimmed eyes focused on Finley. "You said you didn't do it and I believe you."

"Okay, then," Finley said reluctantly, almost grudgingly.

"The animal shelter," Gabe repeated.

Finley nodded. "I'll get the number and call now."

"If she's there, tell them I'll be right over to pick her up." Michelle turned to Gabe. "Sasha is so friendly sometimes people don't realize how sensitive she is and how easily she gets upset."

A stricken look crossed Finley's face. "I hope she's not scared."

For a second, Gabe thought his daughter was going to cry. He placed a hand on her shoulder, praying this would have a happy ending for all their sakes. "I can make the call if—"

"No, I'll do it," Finley spoke quickly. "I—I want to help."

"Everything will be okay," Gabe told Michelle. "Can I get you a glass of iced tea?"

"Do you have something stronger?" Michelle retorted and he chuckled.

Seconds later, Finley returned, a broad smile on her face. "They have her."

"Ohmigod, thank you both." Michelle flung her arms first around Gabe, then around Finley.

Finley gently extricated herself from the hug. "I didn't do anything."

"Yes, you did." Michelle's gaze shifted to Gabe. "Both of you were so supportive. Thank you. Really. Thank you."

"How about we take you to the animal shelter?" Gabe offered. "I believe we'd all like to see for ourselves she's okay."

"If you don't mind driving, I'd appreciate it." Michelle gave a little laugh. "My hands are still shaking. I don't think they're going to stop until I see her."

"You two go," Finley said. "I'll stay here."

"Are you sure?" Gabe asked.

"I—I don't want to see her in a cage." Finley

gazed down at her hands. "Besides, Michelle is the one she'll be eager to see."

"I still think—" Gabe began, but Michelle touched his arm.

"It's okay," Michelle said. "I understand what Finley is saying, but I'm going to bring her over here to see you when we get home."

"You don't have to do that—"

"I want to," Michelle said firmly. "You've been such a good friend to both me and Sasha. It's the least I can do."

On the way home from the animal shelter, Gabe took Michelle's hand. She made no attempt to pull away. Sasha was sleeping in the backseat. All was right in her world.

"I'm sorry I was such a baby earlier." Heat crept up her neck as she recalled her earlier behavior. "When I found out Sasha was gone, I lost it."

"There's no need to apologize." Gabe's fingers tightened around hers. "Finley and I understand how much you love her."

Michelle felt the warmth of his touch all the way up her arm. She tried to ignore the sensation and focus on the conversation. "I think your daughter loves Sasha almost as much as I do. I feel bad about accusing her."

"She understands," Gabe said. "And you apologized. Don't give it another thought."

"It was nice of her to give me this time alone with Sasha."

"You're not completely alone," Gabe reminded her. "I'm with you."

"Tonight made me realize how grateful I am for our friendship." Michelle grew pensive. "You're lucky to have Finley. It's not easy going through life alone."

"I am lucky," he agreed. "But being alone is a choice."

She gave a little laugh. "Please don't tell me you're going to bring up finding me a man."

"No." He reached over and caressed her cheek with the back of his hand. "I simply want to remind you the answers to many problems can often be found right next door."

"I told you Sasha would be fine." Satisfaction filled Addie's voice. "Tell me about Michelle. How did she act?"

Finley pressed the phone more firmly against her ear. Even though her dad was in the living room and she was in her bedroom with the door shut, she kept her voice low. "Stressed to the max. She was crying and everything."

"I bet that was a big turn off for your dad." Finley could almost see Addie wrinkle her nose. "Runny nose, red eyes, slobbering all over. Yuck."

"He hugged her."

"In front of you?" Addie's voice rose and cracked. "No way."

"She got the front of his shirt all wet." When Michelle had cried, Finley had wanted to cry, too. But she wasn't about to reveal that to Addie. "Dad didn't seem to mind."

"Just like we thought, he's got it bad for her."

Finley hated to admit her friend was right, so she remained silent.

"Did she do anything crazy?" Addie asked when the silence lengthened, a hopeful note in her voice.

"Not really." Finley thought for a moment. "She accused me of leaving the gate open, but then apologized."

"Are you telling me her inner she-devil didn't come out at all?"

Finley found herself shaking her head, then realized Addie couldn't see her. "She was just really, really worried about Sasha. It made me feel like pond scum."

"Remember, nothing happened to Sasha other than she had a fun adventure. She'll be babied now because Michelle will be so happy to have her home."

"What if Michelle ends up marrying my dad? How's she going to feel when she discovers this was all a setup? She'll hate me forever."

"Well, for starters, she's not going to find out."

Addie spoke with a confidence Finley envied. "We'll lay low for a while."

Finley expelled a breath she didn't realize she'd been holding. She'd worried Addie might press for another test. "That sounds like a good idea."

"In the meantime, just remember that everything Michelle does and says will reveal her true character. All you have to do is pay attention."

## *Chapter Eleven*

The week passed quickly. Gabe had planned to take Finley hiking and then to the shootout in Town Square on Saturday until she reminded him about the lock-in at the church. Finley told him he'd signed the permission slip, but when she mentioned the entire youth group would be spending the night at the church—including the boys—Gabe had dug in his heels.

He'd immediately called the youth group leader to tell him Finley wouldn't be coming. The youth leader had done his best to reassure Gabe that the kids would be closely chaperoned at all times. Still, his unease persisted. When Finley told him Addie's parents weren't worried at all, Gabe called Nick.

His friend confirmed everything the youth leader had said and assured him that he and Lexi knew the chaperones personally and trusted them. Only then had Gabe given his okay.

But that meant he was on his own today. Unless he asked a friend to spend the day with him. Or perhaps a neighbor…

Gabe had already dropped off Finley at the church and was getting home when he saw Michelle and Sasha down the street heading his way.

The temperature was in the mid-fifties, but the breeze from the north made it feel much colder. Michelle must not have listened to the forecast because her white shorts and tiny blue T were clearly designed for temperatures twenty degrees warmer.

With bright pink cheeks and artfully disheveled

hair, she reminded him of a woman who'd just tumbled out of bed after a night of lovemaking.

His gaze dropped from her full lips to linger on the tight points of her voluptuous breasts. As she drew close, he forced his eyes upward and tried to act casual.

The amused look in her eyes made him wonder if mind reading was another of her attributes.

"Where were you off to so early?" Michelle asked in lieu of a greeting. "I was just getting Sasha's leash when I heard your truck leave."

"I took Finley to the church. They're having a lock-in." The word still felt odd on his tongue.

She laughed. "You sound as if you don't quite know what that is."

He hadn't realized just how blue her eyes were until that moment. A deep vivid blue with little gold specks. The sunlight played on her hair making them look like strands of gold.

"You're right. I'd never heard of such a thing." Gabe frowned, still not sold on the idea. "But I called the youth leader and then spoke with

Nick. I hope I made the right decision letting her attend."

Raising Finley to adulthood was a responsibility Gabe took seriously. It wasn't easy being the sole decision maker. At least in two-parent households you had another adult to steer you back in the right direction if you were becoming too lenient or too strict.

"Our church had lock-ins at least once a year when I was growing up." Michelle's eyes took on a faraway look. From the way her lips curved upward, he could tell the memories she was recalling were pleasant ones. "Most youth leaders use the time to teach the kids how to find practical ways to apply their faith. And it's done in a fun, relaxed atmosphere."

Deepening her faith while being part of a group of like-minded teens was exactly what Gabe wanted for Finley. "Thank you."

A startled look crossed her face. "For what?"

"You've made me feel better about my decision to let her go."

The knowledge that she'd helped Gabe in his parenting duties sent warmth rushing through Michelle.

This was the kind of dialogue she'd envisioned when she married Ed. While she hadn't expected to jump into the mother role with both feet, she had hoped to ease some of Ed's burden by offering another perspective.

It wasn't until after they were married that she realized he didn't want her input. In fact, shortly after the wedding, he'd reassured his daughters that nothing would change in terms of parenting. He would continue to make all decisions. If they had any questions about what they could or couldn't do, they would come to him.

Looking back, she conceded he was probably trying to minimize the impact to the girls of having a stepmother. Yet, his directive had negatively impacted her relationship with Chrissy and Ann. Because their father hadn't valued her input, they didn't either.

"I meant that as a compliment." Gabe touched

her arm and she could see her silence had worried him.

Michelle smiled and changed the subject. "Isn't it a glorious day?"

"Great day for a hike and a shootout."

Michelle cocked her head.

"The shootout in Town Square." Gabe bent down to pet Sasha, who sat at Michelle's side, tail thumping, patiently waiting for him to notice her. "I realize it's a tourist kind of thing, but it'd be fun to see. Because the show isn't until six, I thought I'd do some hiking this afternoon. But I have to admit neither is much fun alone."

"Is that a backhanded invitation?" The second the words left her mouth, Michelle wished she could pull them back. If he wanted to invite her, he'd have asked her to go with him.

"And I thought I was being subtle," Gabe said with a teasing smile. "What do you say? Hiking. Shootout. Dinner?"

*Not a good idea,* the tiny voice of reason in her head whispered.

But with the sun shining brightly and the whole day stretched before her, what he suggested sounded infinitely more appealing than spending the day at home...alone.

"Sounds good. But first I have an errand to run," she said. "I have to stop by and check on the cabin. You can come with me if you like."

"You own a cabin?"

Michelle heard the surprise in his voice. And no wonder. The price of real estate in Jackson Hole had soared in recent years. She'd have to be very wealthy to afford both a condo and a cabin.

On the way to the base of Snow King Mountain, Michelle explained the situation. The cabin they would be visiting was on a long-term lease to a physician recruitment company. The recruiter who'd brought Michelle to Jackson Hole had given her a key and told her to use it whenever she wanted. All she asked was that Michelle check on it once a month to make sure it was being properly maintained.

Michelle smiled as Gabe pulled the truck to a

stop in front of number 10. She loved not only the cabin but also the idyllic setting. Wildflowers edged the walk leading to the log-style structure. Two wooden rocking chairs strategically positioned on the porch afforded a great view of the mountains.

Every couple of weeks she came here to cast off the worries and cares of the outside world and simply relax. It was here that she could truly be herself.

"This is nice," Gabe said before she'd even unlocked the door.

"Just wait." Even though the cabin wasn't hers, Michelle couldn't keep the pride from her voice.

Once inside, Gabe stared in awe at the massive stone fireplace and the antler chandelier hanging over the mission-style table. A low whistle slipped past his lips.

The place was not only beautiful but also immaculate. Michelle couldn't see even a trace of dust on the granite countertops or the hardwood floors. And the floor-to-ceiling windows in the back of the cabin sparkled.

"There are two bedrooms and the sofa is a sleeper," she explained, doing a quick inspection of the smaller one containing two nicely made twin beds before moving on to the master.

This room with its lace curtains hanging at the windows and its own bath was clearly the larger of the two. Michelle strolled to the double bed with the antique white cotton duvet, and ran her hand along the iron frame.

Gabe's eyes never left her hand. "It's so quiet in here."

Michelle nodded, inhaling the soothing scent of lavender from the potpourri on the nightstand. The blinds were open just enough to let bits of golden sunshine bathe the room in natural light. Any remaining tension slid from her shoulders. "Almost like another world."

"But is the bed comfortable?"

The question seemed to come out of left field. Even though she'd spent many days here, because of the need to get back home to Sasha, she couldn't remember the last time she spent the night. She wished, for not the first time, that the management company allowed pets.

Michelle turned and sat down, being careful not to rumple the bedcover. She flattened her hand against the mattress and felt a slight give. "Feels good to me."

Gabe crossed the room and surprised her by sitting next to her, the bed dipping slightly with his weight. He bounced slightly up and down. "Feels about right, but it's hard to tell by just sitting on it."

The moment her eyes touched his, something inside her seemed to lock into place and she couldn't look away. Electricity sizzled in the air. Her heart began to pound.

"I suppose we could lie down," Michelle said in an offhanded tone that gave no indication to the sudden quivering in her throat. "For a second."

With amber eyes looking darker in the dim light, Gabe paused. For a second she was sure he'd say they were acting crazy. She'd laughingly agree and they'd head out the door for their hike.

"We should take off our shoes," he said instead.

She gave a jerky nod. As she slipped off hers, he pulled off his boots, then stretched out on the bed, patting the spot next to him. "Check it out."

Michelle was suddenly reminded of a time in sixth grade when she'd climbed to the third tower at her local swimming pool. When she'd stared at the water so far away, part of her had yearned to run straight back down the ladder to safety. But her more adventurous side had been willing to take a chance on getting hurt for the thrill of free-falling.

Just like then, she couldn't back out now. Of course, she might be reading way too much into the situation. They were both fully dressed. This would really be no different than lying next to him on the deck of a swimming pool. Except right now they had on more clothes.

Yet when Michelle slowly eased herself down beside him and he slipped an arm around her shoulders pulling her comfortably close, she realized a bed and the deck of a pool, where you were surrounded by people, were profoundly different.

"I'm sure you already know this, but I'm very attracted to you," she heard him murmur, his finger tenderly pushing back a lock of hair from her cheek.

Even as Michelle shivered beneath his touch, she found herself holding her breath.

"Moving here was a big step for Finley and me," he continued in the same sexy masculine rumble. "I want to give my job the attention it deserves and also have the time to give Finley whatever help and support she needs to make this a smooth transition."

Was this his way of saying he didn't want a relationship with her? Which was perfect, right? She didn't want to get involved with him either.

"I'm not looking for a relationship with you, not in the traditional sense," Michelle murmured, wondering at the disappointment coursing through her. "Though I do have to admit that I find you very, um, sexy."

He stared at her for a long moment, his eyes boring into hers. "I find you incredibly sexy."

Danger. Danger. The red flags were not only popping up, but they were also waving wildly. Michelle barely noticed. She was more focused on Gabe, the way his shirt clung to his broad chest and that spicy cologne that made her shiver every time she inhaled.

He leaned toward her and lowered his voice. "Do you miss it?"

"Miss what?"

"Sex."

It showed how far gone she was that his question seemed perfectly appropriate. If they'd been anywhere but here, she'd probably tell him it was none of his business. But this room was like a different world where outside parameters didn't apply.

"I do," Michelle admitted. "But I'm not into one-night stands."

"This wouldn't have to be a one-time thing." Gabe trailed a finger up her arm, his smile slow and lazy. "The way I see it, we could do it as much and as often as it worked out."

A shiver of desire traveled up her arm, then took a delicious dip down her spine. "Are you propositioning me, Mr. Davis?"

With a not-quite-steady smile, Gabe nodded, his expression sheepish. "I guess I am."

His husky admission made her blood feel like warm honey sliding through her veins.

"I wouldn't even know how to start an…an affair." Because that's what he was suggesting, right? Heat rose up Michelle's neck. Could he hear her heart pounding? "For example, would we come up with some ground rules first? Like no whips and chains?"

A startled look crossed his face before he grinned. "Agreed."

"Do we just take off our clothes and go at it? Or do we—"

"Shh." His fingers closed over her lips, stopping her nervous babbling. "I'd say we start with a kiss."

His eyes searched hers and Michelle found herself nodding.

Without saying another word, his lips were on hers, exquisitely gentle and achingly tender. His hand flattened against her lower back, drawing her up against the length of his body. A smoldering spark of need flared through her, a sensation she didn't bother to fight.

He took it slow, as if they had all the time in the world. As if no one existed but the two of them. As if nothing else mattered. The room took on a golden glow and the invisible web of attraction tightened around them.

Gabe slid his tongue along her lips and when she opened her mouth, he deepened the kiss. He tasted like the most delicious, decadent candy she'd ever eaten. And she wanted more.

As he continued to kiss her, Michelle found herself running her hands under his shirt.

His muscles were strong and well-corded, just

as she'd imagined. He smelled of soap and that indefinable male scent that made her body ache. Desire, hot and insistent, and for so long forgotten, surged.

"You know it's not fair." He moved his mouth from her lips to the sensitive skin under her jaw.

"What's not fair?" Her voice was raspy and barely recognizable.

"That you can put your hand inside my shirt but I can't do the same to you."

While he spoke, his long fingers lifted and supported her yielding flesh, teasing the tight points of her nipples through the fabric of her shirt.

Her breasts strained against the confining fabric, eager for his touch. "Who, who, says you can't?"

"You're beautiful." He breathed the word as he pushed her shirt up and pressed a warm moist kiss against her bare abdomen. "I want you so much."

Shock waves of desire coursed through her body. In seconds, his clothes hit the floor along with hers. She didn't have time to be embarrassed because he continued to kiss her with a slow thoroughness that left her weak, trembling and longing for more.

Then his lips closed over her breast, his tongue circling the tip before he pulled it in his mouth and sucked. His slow sensual ministrations stoked the flames burning inside her.

She rubbed against him and felt his hardness jump against her belly. Michelle gripped his muscular backside, pulling him to her, wanting him inside her.

His mouth moved lower, then lower still, as his fingers played with her breasts.

"Open," he said in a low husky voice she barely recognized and she let her knees fall apart.

Pushing them even farther apart with his arms, he pressed an open-mouthed intimate kiss between her legs before his fingers slid inside her. First one, then two, the in-and-out motion bringing her near the edge.

"More," she heard herself say, "I want more."

He lifted his head and swore under his breath. "I didn't bring protection."

"I'm on the Pill." She cupped his face with her hand and looked him in the eye. "And I'm clean."

Gabe grinned and gave her a swift kiss. "Looks like there's nothing stopping us now."

Other than good sense, and Michelle wasn't about to go looking for that now.

Just when she thought she couldn't stand waiting a second longer, he entered her. He paused and their eyes met.

"It's big," she said. "I like it."

He kissed her on the lips. "You say the sweetest things."

When she laughed, his breath caught and he began to move. In and out, in and out, slow deliberate thrusts that rubbed her in the best way possible. She clung to him, urging him deeper.

She wanted more, wanted this, wanted him. The kisses became more urgent, their rhythm fevered until the pressure surged and she couldn't hold on any longer. The orgasm hit her with the force of a mighty wave and Michelle cried out as it took her to a place she'd never gone before.

Still Gabe continued to stroke long and slow and deep as if waiting until he was sure he'd wrung out the last bit of pleasure from her, before he shuddered in her embrace and called out her name.

They remained like that for a long while, joined together. Finally Gabe gently pushed her hair off her face. "While we're here we might as well check out the shower."

The gleam in his eyes told her he had more in mind than rinsing off. Which was good, because something more was exactly on her mind, too.

## Chapter Twelve

"You're in a good mood today," Finley told Gabe when she caught him whistling while loading the dishwasher.

Gabe paused, plate in hand. It was almost the same comment that Joel had made at breakfast after church.

"I'm just happy to have you home." He shot his daughter a wink, then added another pan to the rack.

Once he'd picked Finley up from the lock-in, they'd returned home and he made vegetable macaroni and cheese, one of her favorites. She'd had given him a step-by-step account of everything that had gone on at the lock-in before they'd moved on to discuss a dystopian young adult novel they were both reading.

Even though Gabe normally loved these father-daughter times, he had to admit he was having trouble focusing. His mind kept replaying yesterday's events. He couldn't wait to see Michelle again.

He frowned. Had she mentioned a next time? Surely this hadn't been a one-time thing?

"Now it's your turn. Tell me everything you did yesterday," Finley urged. "I like hearing about your day, too."

Gabe started to tell her it was nothing that would interest her, but stopped himself just in time. The last thing he wanted to do was shut down these chats with his daughter.

"After I dropped you off, I washed my car, then I ran into Michelle. We went hiking, then we saw Tripp at the shootout and we all went to dinner. I don't know if I told you but Joel and I are going to be building a stable for Tripp's father."

Finley's eyes lit up. "They have horses?"

Gabe smiled. He knew horses would divert her attention from the fact that he and Michelle had spent the day together. "Lots of them. I mentioned to Tripp that you like to ride and he invited us to come out anytime."

Finley let out a shriek loud enough to be heard at the end of the block. "When can we go? Do you think it'd be okay if we brought Addie? Maybe this weekend. I could check with Addie and see if she's ever ridden. But if she hasn't I don't think it would be that hard for her to pick up the basics, do you?"

"Addie seems like the type who'd catch on quickly." Gabe hid his amusement at his daughter's over-the-top enthusiasm. "I'll be seeing Tripp again Tuesday night. A bunch of us are going to Wally's Place after work. I'll ask him then."

"Is Michelle going?"

"I'm not sure who will show up." Gabe kept his tone offhand and added another plate to the dishwasher rack. "Why do you ask?"

"If Michelle isn't coming right home, she might need someone to walk Sasha that night."

"You've been walking her a lot lately."

"Yeah, but I don't mind." Finley lifted one shoulder in a slight shrug. "Sasha and I are buds. I don't miss Buttercup quite as much when I'm with her."

"Once we get more settled and know how busy you'll be with school and your activities, we should consider getting a dog."

Finley's eyes widened. "Are you serious?"

He knew why she was shocked. After Buttercup had passed on, he'd said no more animals. But now that seemed shortsighted. After all, Finley loved animals. She should have a dog. As long as they could be sure they had the time to give it the attention it deserved.

"Oh, Daddy, you're the best." Finley flung her

arms around Gabe's neck and gave him a bear hug. "This has been the best weekend ever."

"Yes, it has, Finley." He kissed the top of her head. "Indeed it has."

Tuesday night, Michelle stood on the sidewalk outside Wally's Place, dressed in her favorite skinny jeans, trying to decide if she wanted to go inside or not. Several friends, Adrianna being one of them, had invited her to this get-together tonight. Wally's Place was a popular sports bar in Jackson. It had everything any cowgirl or cowboy could want: sawdust and peanut shells on the floor, a mechanical bull—that Michelle had vowed never to go near—and the best burgers in town.

But it wasn't food or concerns about the atmosphere that was making her hesitate, it was the knowledge that Gabe would likely be there. This would be the first time she'd seen him since Saturday night and she wasn't sure how to act.

She thought she'd run into him at church Sunday, but a patient with a ruptured ectopic pregnancy had put her in surgery all morning.

The truth was, she felt rather shy about seeing him. It wasn't embarrassment over what had gone on in the cabin as much as it was insecurity over where they went from here.

They'd done more kissing than talking that day. It wasn't until afterward that she realized they'd never really addressed what came next.

Since that night she found herself glancing at his home and wondering if he was thinking of her. She felt like a schoolgirl with a massive crush on the boy next door. Of course, she reminded herself, she and Gabe didn't have a relationship and he wouldn't be taking her to the prom.

The Emily Post question of the day was, how to react to him in public? They'd agreed to keep their sexual relationship completely private. That much they *had* discussed. But should she—

"If you're standing there waiting for someone to open the door, I'm your man."

Michelle jerked her head up and found Tripp

grinning at her, one hand on the large ornate door handle leading into Wally's Place.

"My knight in shining armor." Michelle pulled her thoughts back to the present and returned his smile. "I've been waiting a long time for you."

"Ah, Michi, you make my heart go pitter-patter with those sweet words." She thought about taking him to task for using her nickname, but instead she just laughed.

In fact, he entertained her so thoroughly that by the time they reached the tables where their friends were congregated, Michelle realized her hand was still wrapped around Tripp's arm in a very familiar manner.

She wasn't the only one who noticed. Even though he called out a warm greeting, Gabe's eyes narrowed ever so slightly. And a stricken look filled Adrianna's beautiful eyes for a split second before she recovered.

"There are a couple seats over here." Adrianna's calm demeanor and cool tone gave nothing away.

Gabe on the other hand looked ready to break a board with his bare hands. His gaze shifted from Tripp to Michelle. "You two come together?"

"No," Tripp responded before Michelle could form the words. "I rescued Michelle outside."

"Rescued?" Adrianna's eyes widened and her gaze shot to Michelle. "What happened? Are you okay?"

Michelle rolled her eyes. "What Tripp meant to say is he opened the door for me when we ran into each other outside."

"Must you always be so literal?" Tripp shook his head in disgust. "You're no fun."

Michelle eyes met Gabe's. The look in those amber depths said he thought she was a whole lot of fun. And that he was glad she hadn't come with Tripp.

Perhaps if she was thinking rationally, she'd have been worried that Gabe seemed a little, well, possessive. Instead it warmed her heart.

"Have you ordered yet?" Michelle glanced at the menus scattered on the table.

"Ryan and I got here first," Betsy explained. "We ordered several pizzas for everyone to share."

The waitress came and took their drink orders. Michelle chatted with Lexi and Ryan and Tripp, all the while wishing that she'd gotten there a little earlier so she would be sitting closer to Gabe.

Until, of course, she came to her senses and realized the seating arrangement was fine just the way it was. Because if she was sitting next to Gabe—as Betsy was—it would be too easy to touch him, which was what she wanted to do.

"Did you see Finley tonight?" Michelle asked Gabe when there was a lull in the conversation. She'd texted his daughter from the hospital and the girl had agreed to feed Sasha and take her for a walk.

"As a matter of fact, I stopped by Nick's house after work, picked up Addie and dropped her off at home. The girls planned to make grilled cheese for dinner, then take Sasha for a long walk. They told me to stay out as long as I liked."

Michelle licked her suddenly dry lips. Unless she was reading too much into his words, he'd just told her he was free for the evening…and with Finley watching Sasha, she was, too.

"I'll probably have a piece of pizza and then head…out," she said, toying with the top button of her white shirt.

His eyes darkened. "I'm not staying long either. There's a place I still need to check out tonight."

Michelle wondered if that place was a cabin at the base of Snow King Mountain. She hoped so, because once she left Wally's Place, that's where she was going…to wait for him.


The sound of a truck motor coming down the road sent Michelle's heart into high gear. According to her watch she'd been waiting for about fifteen minutes—though it seemed like a couple of hours—hoping Gabe would show up.

In her mind, the signals had been clear, but she worried she'd read too much into what could have been simply a few innocent comments. Then a familiar red pickup pulled in front of the cabin and Michelle realized she and Gabe had been on the same wavelength.

She rose from the rocking chair where she'd been sitting and smiled. "I wasn't sure you were coming."

"It took me longer to get away than I thought." Gabe stepped onto the porch. "Once everyone decided to play darts, I was able to slip away."

"I'm glad." Michelle wound her arms around his neck and planted a kiss at the base of his throat, his skin salty beneath her lips.

He pulled her tight against his body, so close she could feel his heart beating. "I can't stop thinking about you."

"I brought condoms." When she grabbed a handful from the clinic's supply closet, she'd promised herself if this…affair…continued, the next time she was in Idaho Falls she'd buy some to replace the ones she'd taken. "Just to be extra safe."

"Great minds think alike." He grinned. "I brought some, too."

Michelle's hands moved to the buttons of his shirt. "In that case we should be covered for—"

She frowned as he gently pulled her hands down.

"It's a beautiful evening," he said. "How about a walk?"

"A walk?" Her eyes, which seemed to suddenly develop a mind of their own, zeroed in on the area directly below his belt buckle.

He caught her hand in his, lifted it to his mouth and pressed a kiss in the palm. "Humor me. Please."

What could she say but okay?

Michelle locked the door. She'd just slipped the key to the cabin into her pocket when Gabe held out his hand.

"Why, Mr. Davis—" Michelle used her best southern accent "—I never knew you liked to hold hands."

"There's a lot you don't know about me." Gabe

winked and then smiled when she let him take her hand.

"That's okay." Michelle forced an easy-breezy tone. "All I care about is your body."

His smile never faltered but something flickered in his eyes.

They strolled into the woods hand-in-hand. Michelle told herself she should be proud she'd made it clear where their relationship stood. Instead of feeling as if she'd somehow shortchanged them both.

They'd been walking for several minutes when he reached out and pulled her close. Michelle felt a surge of excitement. She'd never made love outdoors before. God help her, she batted her lashes at him, felling like a shameless wanton. "What do you have in mind?"

He directed his gaze to her feet.

Michelle glanced down and found a log almost completely covered in green foliage. Heat flared up her neck as she realized she'd totally misread the situation. "Thanks. Looks like you saved me from a fall."

Gabe brushed a kiss against her jaw, then whispered in her ear, "I won't let anything hurt you."

Was he talking about her ankles or her heart?

They strolled slowly through the trees, the branches like an umbrella overhead. Other than an occasional chirp from a bird and a squirrel's noisy chatter, all was quiet. Michelle wondered if she'd appear too eager if she suggested they forget communing with nature and head back to the cabin.

"Tell me about your first kiss."

For a second Michelle wasn't sure she'd heard correctly. "Beg pardon?"

"Tell me about your first kiss," he repeated. "Be specific. Tell me how old you were, what he did, all of it."

"Seriously? You want to talk about kissing?"

He nodded. Even though his expression was solemn, there was an odd gleam in his eyes.

"Hoo-kay." Michelle smiled. Did any woman

forget her first kiss? "Tommy was my next-door neighbor."

"That should have been your first warning." Gabe chuckled. "You've got to watch out for neighbors."

Michelle stopped walking and leaned back against a tree. "I was fifteen. He was seventeen." She leveled a glance at Gabe. "Remember this when Finley gets in high school. You have to watch those older boys."

"It was just a kiss."

"He slipped his hand inside my shirt."

Gabe's eyes widened. "He jumped to second base?"

"I believe his goal was to hit a home run." Michelle's lips lifted in a wry smile. "My father's unexpected return home put an end to that fantasy."

"You'd have stopped him, anyway."

"Perhaps." Michelle batted her eyes at Gabe. "You have to understand, Tommy was a real hunk."

"And he knew all the right words." Gabe looked her up and down. "I bet he started with compliments like 'You're the most beautiful girl I know.'"

The words were said with such sincerity that warmth returned to Michelle's veins and she felt herself begin to relax.

"Your hair is like spun silk," Gabe continued in the same low seductive tone. "Your eyes are as blue as the ocean. I feel myself drowning each time I look in them."

Her breath stalled, then began again as his gaze dropped to her mouth. "Your lips are like ripe strawberries. Sweet and soft."

Michelle couldn't have taken her eyes from his if she tried. And that husky rasp to his voice made her tingle all over. "Th-thank you," she managed to murmur.

He reached up and gathered her close to him. "Do you know what I've wanted to do all night?"

By now she'd stopped breathing. She shook her head from side to side, her eyes wide.

"Kiss you." With one finger he traced the shape of her lips. "Is it okay if I kiss you, Michi?"

There was a beat of silence.

"Please." She forced the word past her suddenly dry throat.

He slipped his fingers through her hair, cupping her head, then lowering his mouth to hers. The kiss started out slow and sweet, but then his tongue slipped past her lips and the intensity kicked up several notches.

His hand slid up her sides stopping to rest the tips of his fingers just below her breasts.

Even though he continued to kiss her, his fingers never covered those last few centimeters. She shimmied trying to show him she wanted more. More kissing, more touching. But instead of more, he took a step back and his hand dropped to his side. "Time to go back to the cabin."

"Aren't you going to kiss me again?"

A half smile pulled up his lips. "Sweetheart, I'm going to do a whole lot more than kiss you," he said, pulling her along.

"But we didn't even talk about *your* first kiss," Michelle protested.

A corner of his mouth twitched. "You really feel like talking?"

Just for fun, Michelle thought about saying yes. But she was afraid he might take her up on it. So she just shook her head and continued with the frantic pace through the trees. "Next time."

He smiled. "Yeah, next time."

## Chapter Thirteen

Michelle had barely gotten home from the cabin when she was called into the hospital for a difficult birth. By the time she returned to her condo, it was close to three in the morning. Thankfully tomorrow was Saturday and unless another baby chose to come into the world in the next two days, she had the weekend to herself.

As she pulled back the sheets and plumped up the pillow, she found herself wishing Gabe were there so she could tell him all about the baby girl who'd been determined to make her entrance into the world as difficult as possible. The second the thought crossed her mind, she realized just how thoroughly her neighbor had become a part of her life.

For just a few seconds she let herself dream what it'd be like if Gabe were unencumbered. If she could get as close as she wanted and hold on tight. But he was a father with full custody of a teenage daughter.

Granted, Michelle had grown to like and respect Finley. It made her angry to think of Finley's mother ignoring such a wonderful girl. Why, any woman could be proud to call such an intelligent and sensitive child her daughter.

*Even me?*

For a second Michelle found herself tempted to fully open her heart to Finley and to Gabe. Until she reminded herself she had good reason to keep her distance from both of them. Did she really want a repeat of the fiasco with Ed? *No,* she told herself firmly, *she did not.*

If she was smart, she should distance herself

from Gabe right now. Before he breached the wall she'd erected around her heart. A barrier put up specifically to keep him out.

Yes, she really should—

The thought hadn't completely formed when her cell phone began to buzz. Michelle stifled a groan hoping she didn't have to get dressed and head back to the hospital again.

But when she brought the phone close, she saw Gabe's number. Her heart gave an excited leap.

"Hey, you," she said softly. "What's up?"

"I saw your bedroom light was on," he said in a gravelly voice. "How did it go at the hospital?"

"Mom and baby are doing well." She told herself to keep the conversation brief and to the point. If she could just figure out what was the point. "But it was a tough delivery."

"What happened?"

He sounded so genuinely interested that Michelle went on to explain about the mother's insistence on a vaginal birth even when it appeared a C-section might be necessary.

After letting her talk, Gabe asked several good questions. She was surprised at his familiarity with childbirth until she remembered he'd witnessed it on a very personal level.

"You're a good doctor, Michelle. You really care about your patients."

She settled back against the pillows. "If you don't care, what's the point?"

"Exactly," he said softly, his voice slightly muffled. "And that holds true for almost everything we do in life. If you don't let yourself care, then what is the point?"

"How sick is he?" Addie asked with an eagerness that brought a frown to Finley's brow.

Finley stepped briefly into the living room and narrowed her gaze, taking in her father's pale face with the beads of sweat dotting his forehead. She glanced down at his rumpled shirt and pants. All day he'd been cold, then hot. The floor held the extra blanket he must have tossed off.

He seemed more comfortable sprawled out on

the sofa rather than in bed. The television was tuned to a sports station, but in the past half hour she hadn't seen him look at it once.

"I can't get his fever under one hundred." Finley kept her voice low. "He's hot, then he's cold. And he coughs all the time."

"Good."

"Good?" Finley wasn't sure she'd heard her friend correctly. When she'd called Addie to tell her she couldn't come to her impromptu party, she thought her friend would be more sympathetic.

"Is Michelle home?"

Addie's abrupt change in subject didn't surprise Finley. She'd already learned that her friend's mind zigzagged its way to a destination. Finley moved back to her position in the kitchen. From the window she could see the doctor's back deck where Michelle sat reading a book and sipping a glass of iced tea. "She's there."

"Perfect." There was a couple heartbeats of silence on the other end of the line before Addie spoke again. "Tell your dad the party is to introduce you to kids who will be in your class in the fall. Stress how important this is to you. I'm betting that he'll encourage you—heck, maybe even insist—that you go."

"I can't leave him, Addie." Finley glanced at the sheen of perspiration on her dad's forehead and her heart turned over. "He doesn't have the strength to get up and make himself something to eat. Or even to get a glass of water so he can take his ibuprofen. He looks bad. Really bad. He needs someone to take care of him."

"Of course he does." Addie's voice trembled with excitement. "And this will be the perfect opportunity to see if Michelle is the type of person to rise to the challenge."

Finley stilled. "Are you saying this would be another test?"

"Absolutely. Surely you don't want your dad with a person who could walk away from him in his hour of need."

"But that's what I'd be doing," Finley protested.

"Dad and I, we take care of each other. When I had chicken pox, he missed a big test at school. How can I leave him now?"

"Well…" Addie didn't say anything for several seconds. "Think of it this way. It won't be long until you're away at college. What if he marries Michelle and you find out she won't take care of him when he's sick? What are you going to do then?"

"She's a doctor," Finley reminded her friend. "Of course she'd take care of him."

"She takes care of ladies who are having babies," Addie pointed out. "That doesn't mean she'll take care of your dad."

"You're right," Finley reluctantly conceded.

"It's up to you," Addie said, her voice softening. "But doing this is necessary."

Finley knew Addie believed what she was saying made sense. But to leave her dad here alone… What if Michelle didn't come through? Her heart clenched. "I don't think she even knows that he's sick."

"Then make sure and mention that fact to her before you leave," Addie said in a matter-of-fact tone.

Finley told herself she had to do this, that she really didn't have a choice. "Okay, but you have to promise you'll bring me home when I ask. I don't want to leave him alone too long."

"We'll be there in a half hour to pick you up."

Finley clicked off the phone, shaking off her unease. This wouldn't be the last time her father got sick. She had to be certain that before she left for college he had someone who cared enough to be there for him through the good times…and the bad.

Michelle found it odd when Finley stopped over to inform her that not only was her dad ill, but that she was going to Addie Delacourt's house for a party.

Yesterday, when Kate Dennes had come in for a follow-up check, she'd told Michelle there'd been some kind of respiratory flu going around the job site and was worried about Joel bringing it home. She'd also mentioned Gabe had called in sick that morning.

But if he was sick enough to stay home yesterday, what was Finley doing leaving him? Unless…having Finley mention she was leaving was Gabe's way of telling her the coast was clear and Michelle should come over.

Her lips curved up in a smile. Yes, that had to be it. After putting on some lip gloss and running a brush through her hair, she headed next door. She knocked several times, but when Gabe didn't come to the door, she tried the knob. Unlocked.

Pushing the door open, she called out, "It's Michelle. Is it okay if I come in?"

"Yes." The single word was followed by a coughing fit.

Michelle stepped into the living room. She didn't see Gabe at first. Finally she spotted a tuft of dark hair over the top of the sofa.

When she got to his side, she gasped. Like a train wreck, Michelle couldn't look away.

Dark circles underpinned Gabe's eyes and the skin under his cheek stubble had a ghostly sheen. His hair stuck up at odd angles. A tissue box and a glass of water sat on the coffee table in front of him.

His eyes were red-rimmed and bloodshot. "I don't feel much like doing anything."

"Well, of course you don't." She made a sympathetic sound. "I'm sure sitting on the sofa is about as much as you can manage."

"No," he choked out. "I mean like at the cabin…"

Whatever else he'd been about to say was cut off by a fit of coughing. She finally realized what he was trying to tell her. Despite her worry, the thought pulled a smile from her.

"I'm not here for sex, mister." Michelle dropped down in the chair next to the sofa, the original reason for her visit forgotten. "I came to see how you're feeling."

"I've been better." Gabe reached for a glass of water, nearly knocking it over.

"Let me help you with that." Taking the glass Michelle crouched down by the sofa and lifted the crystal tumbler to his lips. "Small sips," she said when he drank greedily. She resisted the urge to push the straggling hair back from his face. "When did you last have some Tylenol?"

"I don't know." He lifted a hand to rub his forehead. "Finley has been keeping track."

*Finley.* The daughter who'd deserted him to go to a party with her friends. Michelle kept her mouth shut and mentally counted to ten. When she finally spoke, her tone was calm and matter-of-fact, not condemning. "Did she write it down?"

"I think so. I'm not sure." He shook his head as if hoping to clear it.

Michelle pulled her brows together. "Where do you keep the Tylenol?"

"In the kitchen. The cabinet by the sink."

"Let me see if there's any kind of record in there." Michelle patted him awkwardly on the shoulder. "I'll be right back."

She found a list by the sink, along with bottles of both Tylenol and ibuprofen and a thermometer. It wasn't time yet for another dose of ibuprofen, but he could certainly handle some more Tylenol after she checked his temperature. She picked up the old-fashioned thermometer and carried it with her into the living room.

"Did you find it?" He didn't bother lifting his head from the pillow.

"Right where you said it would be." She hid her concern behind a reassuring smile. "First, let's take your temperature."

Obligingly, he opened his mouth.

One hundred one. After giving him the Tylenol, Michelle gave in to impulse and gently pushed that stubborn strand of hair back from his forehead. "How long has it been since you showered?"

Gabe lifted one shoulder in a slight shrug.

"I bet you'd feel better if you did."

"Okay." But when he pushed to his feet he swayed.

"Whoa there, pardner." Michelle wrapped an arm around his waist and steadied him. "Don't go falling on me."

His lips tipped up in the slightest of smiles. "I got up too fast. I'm fine now."

"If you don't mind, I think I'll just walk with you for a little bit. Just to make sure."

They made their way haltingly across the hardwood floor to the doorway to the bathroom. Michelle didn't leave his side until she'd made sure everything he needed was in easy reach. "Leave the door cracked. I want to be able to hear if you need anything."

The first real smile she'd seen since she walked through the door lifted his lips. "You're bossy."

"So I've been told."

He reached out and trailed a finger down her cheek. "I like it."

Michelle gazed into those beautiful amber eyes now dulled with illness. Even at his worst, the guy had a killer smile.

"I'll get some food ready for you."

"Would it matter if I told you I'm not hungry?"

She wrinkled her nose. "Not at all."

Their gazes met. Suddenly it was as if they were the only two people in the world. He breathed. She breathed. Her heart slipped into an irregular rhythm.

The corner of his mouth twitched, breaking the spell. "Yep, definitely bossy."

"That's already been established. Now get in the shower."

Michelle waited near the door until she heard the water turn on. What was Finley thinking, leaving him like this? She pressed her lips together and returned to the kitchen.

The cupboards were surprisingly well-stocked. Because it had been a while since Gabe had eaten, Michelle decided on chicken noodle soup. After thawing several chicken breasts in the microwave, she cut them up, then added them, along with carrots and celery, to chicken broth. When that was done she added the egg noodles to the stock. The soup wasn't quite homemade but it would have to do.

"Smells good." Gabe stood in the doorway, wearing sweatpants and a faded blue T-shirt. His feet were bare and his hair damp.

"Chicken noodle soup." Michelle smiled. "And it's ready to eat."

"You didn't have to go to all this trouble." He shifted from one foot to the other. "But thank you."

The look of gratitude in his eyes brought a lump to her throat. "Take a seat and I'll dish you up some."

"You'll eat with me." It was a statement more than a question.

"If you'd like," she said, feeling suddenly shy.

"I definitely like."

He was feeling better. Michelle could tell by simply looking at him. His cheeks were no longer flushed, telling her the Tylenol had done its job. And there was a gleam in his eyes when he looked at a formfitting T that hadn't been there before the shower.

Simply having him look at her that way made her heart skip a beat. How many days had it been since they'd made love? *Too many,* her body said.

Not that she was entertaining the thought right now, but soon he would be well and then…

"You look a bit flushed." His eyes narrowed with concern. "Are you sure you're not coming down with something?"

She ladled some soup into a bowl and set it before him, then repeated the process for herself. "I feel great. It's probably from slaving over a hot stove."

Gabe settled back into his chair, his blue T-shirt a perfect foil for his dark hair. Hair which was still damp from the shower and artfully disheveled, as if he'd just raked his hand through it.

Something stirred low in her abdomen. *He's sick,* she reminded herself sternly.

Even though she knew he had to be hungry, he didn't pick up his spoon. "Something wrong?"

He smiled. "I'm waiting for you."

Michelle picked up her spoon. "Oh, I get it. You're worried I might have put something in it, so you want me to go first."

"Just being a gentleman, sweetheart," he drawled. "If you'd wanted to do me in all you'd have to have done is ignore me. I was feeling not so good when you arrived, in case you didn't notice."

A rush of warmth washed over Michelle. She liked it that he'd called her sweetheart. Liked it a bit too much in fact. She considered telling him that it wasn't appropriate, but figured they were alone in the house. If he wanted to call her sweetheart, she'd let him. Just this time.

Michelle dipped her spoon into the soup and tasted it. Her lips curved upward.

Following her lead, Gabe did the same. He closed his eyes as he swallowed, an odd look on his face.

"How is it?" Michelle almost hated to ask.

"It's…" Gabe opened his eyes. "Delicious. Heavenly."

Michelle took a little more. It *was* pretty good.

They talked as they ate. She told him about the set of twins who'd weighed eight pounds each that she'd delivered yesterday. He told her about the new stable they'd started building for Tripp's dad.

Gabe glossed over his illness. When Michelle mentioned being surprised that Finley would leave him when he didn't feel well, he rose to his daughter's defense.

In that moment he reminded her of Ed when she'd say something about Chrissy. Nothing was ever his daughter's fault. There was always some excuse for her bad behavior.

A tightness gripped Michelle's chest. Her appetite vanished. She began to rise, but Gabe reached out and pulled her back down.

"Tell me what's going on with Tripp."

Michelle paused and dropped back into her

seat, surprised both by the abrupt change in subject and the question. "What do you mean?"

"At times I'm convinced he wants you," Gabe said in a casual tone that Michelle guessed was anything but casual. "Other times I'm not so sure."

"It's not me, it's Adrianna," Michelle said honestly. "For some reason, he's hesitant about pursuing her. As much as I know she likes him, there's something holding her back, too."

"That's what I thought." Gabe relaxed against the back of his chair.

"What made you think of him?"

"I wasn't thinking of him." Gabe lifted the glass of water from the coffee table. This time, his hand was steady. "I was thinking of you. If there was something between you and him, I needed to know."

"If something was going on with me and another guy, I'd tell you." Michelle paused. "Just like if you started up something with another woman, I trust that you'd tell me."

"Absolutely."

Michelle felt disturbed by his response. Not that she wanted him to say there was no other woman he wanted—that would have sent her running for the hills, er, the mountains—but couldn't he have said something about how good it was between them?

The second the thought entered her mind, she realized how foolish she was being. She couldn't have it both ways. She'd made it perfectly clear she only wanted his friendship and wasn't looking for anything more.

The sound of a car pulling into the driveway brought Michelle to her feet. Seconds later the front door swung open. "Dad, I'm home."

"We're in the kitchen, Finley," Gabe called out.

Michelle barely had time to gather up the dishes when Finley appeared in the doorway. The teen rushed to her dad's side, then crouched down beside him.

"How are you doing?" Finley's anxious gaze scanned his face. Almost immediately the two lines between her brows relaxed. "You look… better."

"I think I'm going to live," he admitted. "Michelle made chicken noodle soup."

"I left the party early specifically so I could make you dinner." Finley appeared put out by the fact that her father had eaten.

*Just like Chrissy,* Michelle thought.

"There's some soup left over." Michelle forced a smile to her lips. "It's still warm. I could get you—"

"I can get it myself." Finley straightened. "This is my house. I think I know my way around it better than you."

"Finley." Gabe's dark eyes flashed. "That was rude."

The skin on the teen's cheeks darkened to a rosy hue. "I'm sorry," she said sounding surprisingly contrite. "That didn't come out right."

"No worries." Michelle waved a dismissive hand. "No offense taken."

But Michelle headed home almost immediately,

ignoring Gabe's protests, telling him she had paperwork waiting for her at home. There had been a promise in Gabe's eyes when he'd said goodbye at the door, a promise that disturbed more than comforted her.

Finley's behavior tonight had served as a timely reminder of the dangers of getting too close to Gabe. It was a warning she was determined to heed.

## Chapter Fourteen

"She left him there, Adrianna." Thought it had been almost a week and Gabe had fully recovered, Michelle's blood began to boil simply thinking of that evening. "She went to a party rather than take care of him."

Adrianna took a tiny bite of her salad. "That upsets you."

"Darn right it does." Michelle lowered her voice when the people at the next table turned to stare. Hill of Beans was crowded and, for all its sophistication, Jackson was still a small town. "Gabe needed Tylenol. He needed food. Finley waltzed out the door as if she didn't care. Totally irresponsible."

"I thought you said she came back specifically to make him dinner."

Michelle cursed the need that had made her give Adrianna all of the details instead of just the relevant ones. "At seven o'clock."

"Lots of people don't eat until seven. Besides, she's thirteen." For some reason the midwife seemed determined to take the girl's side. "It's easy to make bad choices when you're young."

"Really?" Michelle couldn't hide her irritation. "To me, this is an issue of character, not of age."

Adrianna put down her fork. Her lips pressed together and she appeared to be forcibly restraining herself.

"I'd say you appear to be letting your past experience with Ed's daughters color your views of Finley." Adrianna's green eyes flashed. "From what I've seen, she's a nice, caring child. A child, Michelle, not an adult."

"She left her sick dad all alone to go to a party. What kind of person does something like that?"

Adrianna leaned forward, her gaze pinning Michelle to her chair. "Sounds like you never made any mistakes when you were young. Bully for you. But you know as well as I do that it's rare for a person to get through those growing-up years without regrets. Character is developed by how a person deals with adversity, especially adversity brought on by their own bad decisions."

Michelle couldn't remember the last time she'd seen Adrianna so passionate about a topic. She hadn't realized her friend was so fond of Finley. "I'll grant—"

Without her usual fluid grace, Adrianna abruptly stood. "I'm sorry. I just remembered I have a couple of errands to run before my afternoon appointments."

The salad in front of her friend had barely been touched. "Can't it wait until you finish your lunch?"

"No." Adrianna flashed a tight smile. "It can't."

As she watched her friend stride out the door, Michelle had the feeling she'd said something terribly wrong. Worse yet, she sensed what she'd said had hurt Adrianna. But what—

"Couldn't decide what you wanted for lunch?"

Her head jerked up. Tripp stood beside the table, a tray in his hands and a grin on his lips.

"What are you talking about?" she managed to spit out.

"Sandwich." Tripp pointed to the ham-and-Swiss in front of her, then gestured to the salad. "Salad."

"Oh, that's Adrianna's."

Something she couldn't identify flickered in his eyes. He glanced around. "Where is she?"

"She left." Michelle tried to summon a smile but failed. "She had some errands to run."

"Was that before or after she saw me come in?"

"Huh?"

"Never mind." Tripp gestured with his head to the empty chairs at the table. "Do you mind if we join you?"

"We?"

"Gabe and me." Tripp turned and that's when Michelle saw him, holding his own tray of food, weaving his way through the tables.

Even dressed casually in jeans and the standard Stone Craft Builders polo, Gabe cut a fine figure. Several women turned for a second look as he walked past their table.

*Mine.*

The thought took her by surprise and sent waves of shock rippling through her body. But she didn't have time to think any more about it because suddenly he was there, standing beside the table, smiling, his eyes filled with warmth.

"Have a seat," she said, never taking her eyes off Gabe.

"I assume that invitation extends to me, too," Tripp said.

Michelle shifted her gaze. "Of course it does, you goof."

"Did you hear what she called me, Davis?"

Tripp protested. "I'm the hospital administrator. Her superior."

Michelle raised one eyebrow and gave him a long, measuring glance.

"Perhaps that was a poor choice of words." Tripp pulled out a chair and sat down.

Gabe chuckled.

Michelle cleared her throat. Loudly.

"Okay it *was* a poor choice of words and totally not true," Tripp said. "Except the part about my being a hospital administrator. That part is true."

"How's your day going?" Michelle asked Gabe.

"Be careful how you answer, Davis," Tripp warned. "Or Michelle will nail you to the wall. She's in a testy mood."

"I'm in a fabulous mood," Michelle snapped.

"You ran Adrianna off," Tripp pointed out.

Gabe's eyes widened with surprise. "What happened?"

"I didn't run her off." Even to her own ears, Michelle's protest lacked conviction. She still wondered what she'd said that had gotten her friend so upset. "She had errands."

A softness filled Gabe's eyes at the slight tremble to her voice.

Her heart rose to her throat. She shoved it back down.

"What are you two doing here?" Michelle asked, desperate for a change of subject.

"Right now?" Tripp grinned. "Harassing you."

Gabe shot him a quelling glance. "Tripp and I just got back from his father's ranch."

"Dad needs a new stable," Tripp informed her.

"Stable?" Michelle leaned forward, her gaze focused on Tripp. "As in horses?"

"Lots of pretty horses." Tripp appeared amused by her sudden interest. "All different colors and sizes."

"I take it you like to ride?" Gabe asked.

"I do."

"You and Finley have that in common. There was a riding academy not far from where we lived in Philly." A smile lifted Gabe's lips. "Finley took lessons and rode as much as she could."

"Why don't you—" Tripp pointed to Michelle "—and you—" he pointed to Gabe "—come to my dad's place this Saturday afternoon. You can ride, then stay for the barbecue. And of course, bring your daughter."

Gabe glanced at Michelle, a question in his eyes. "Sounds like fun."

Michelle hesitated. "Adrianna and I were planning to go to a movie."

Of course, because of how lunch had gone, those plans might have changed.

"Bring her along," Tripp said.

"You don't mind?"

The hospital administrator looked puzzled. "Why would I?"

Could he really be so clueless over the mixed signals he sent out? "It's just that sometimes I get the feeling that you and she aren't on good terms."

"Adrianna and I are friends," Tripp said, his eyes daring her to disagree.

The safest course seemed to simply smile. "I'll ask her. Unless you want to—"

"You had plans." Tripp wrapped his fingers around the bulging sandwich. "She may still want to go to the movies."

"Maybe," Michelle said vaguely, but she knew that nothing would keep Adrianna away from the barbecue. Even though they'd both deny it, Adrianna and Tripp were drawn together like two powerful magnets. "If I had to guess, I'd say she'll pick horses over a movie."

"Great," Tripp said. "It's a date."

Gabe smiled at Michelle. "Like the man said, it's a date."

"Are you sure it's okay if I come?" Finley asked Gabe for what felt like the millionth time.

But the anxious expression on her face reminded him that everything was a big deal when you were thirteen. And at that age you didn't want to be somewhere you weren't invited.

"Tripp specifically mentioned you," Gabe said over his shoulder as he backed the truck from the garage. "You and Michelle are the horse lovers."

With Michelle going to the same place, it didn't make sense for them to drive separately. Of course he had to promise if Michelle got called to the hospital they'd leave immediately.

"I'm sure she doesn't want me along," Finley said from the backseat while they waited for Michelle to come out.

Gabe turned in his seat toward his daughter. "Why would you say that?"

Finley lifted one thin shoulder in a slight shrug. "I don't think she liked it that I went to Addie's house when you were sick."

"I told you to go," he reminded her gently.

"I know, but I think she thought I should have stayed with you," she mumbled.

"I was fine." Gabe shot his daughter a reassuring smile. Finley had always been such a sensitive child. "I can make sure Michelle understands—"

"No, Dad, no. Do. Not. Say anything to her. Please."

For a second Finley looked as if she was about to cry, which didn't make any sense. Of course, Michelle getting so upset at Hill of Beans the other day hadn't made any sense either. Thinking back, Gabe wondered if Michelle and Adrianna had gotten in some kind of argument.

He'd meant to ask her about it, but the last time they'd planned to get together at the cabin had been postponed. What Michelle called a "precipitous" delivery had demanded her attention.

"Dad." Finley interrupted his thoughts. "She's coming this way. Promise you won't say anything."

"Scout's honor." Gabe lifted his fingers in a familiar salute. In the rearview mirror he saw Finley roll her eyes.

He grinned and hopped out of the truck, reaching the passenger side door at the same time as

Michelle. Dressed simply in jeans, boots and a white button-down cotton shirt open at the neck, she reminded him of a citified cowgirl. A very appealing cowgirl.

"You look nice." He opened the door with a flourish.

Instead of stepping inside, Michelle smiled at Finley, then turned back to him. "I can sit in the back."

"Don't waste your breath." Finley spoke before Gabe could respond. "You're the adult. You sit in front. Those are the rules."

Gabe shot his daughter a warning glance.

"And you're our guest," Finley added hastily.

"Well, thank you," Michelle said to Finley, then turned to Gabe. "Adrianna said she'd meet us there."

"Is the ranch far?" Finley leaned forward while Michelle fastened her seat belt.

By that time Gabe had jumped back behind the wheel. "Fifteen minutes max."

"I hope I remember how to ride." The worried frown was back on Finley's face. "It's been a long time."

"As long as I don't fall off, I'll be happy," Gabe muttered.

"Oh, Dad, you're not *that* klutzy."

"I bet your father is a good rider," Michelle said loyally.

Finley gave a little snort. "Yeah, just wait."

After Gabe's comments, Michelle had been prepared for him to be a tenderfoot. Then she realized she should have known better. The man was too athletic and coordinated to be anything but a good rider.

"I'm going to be so sore tomorrow," Michelle groaned as she repositioned herself on the log bench. She and Gabe had taken a seat around the large fire pit with a group of Tripp's parents' friends.

Gabe lowered his voice for her ears only. "Next time we're alone, I'll give you a massage, guaranteed to ease those sore muscles."

"Shh." Michelle flushed. "Someone will hear you."

"They're too busy comparing surgery stories to pay any attention to us."

Most of the guests Tripp's parents had invited were older. That's why it was no surprise that after a dinner of grilled T-bones and corn on the cob, the talk turned to recent surgeries and doctor's appointments.

"What about Adrianna and Tripp?"

"They seem to be involved in a rather intense conversation." Michelle gestured with her head toward the couple who sat on another bench closer to the fire.

"What do you think they're talking about?"

"No idea." Michelle didn't really want to discuss Adrianna. Things had remained strained between them since the conversation in the coffee shop. She glanced around. "Where's Finley?"

"Playing a game of horse with Tripp's sister up by the house. They have a lighted court."

"I didn't know Tripp had a sister," Michelle

stammered. "Or that Finley liked to play basketball."

"Sounds like there's a lot you don't know," Gabe teased.

"I'm beginning to believe that," Michelle said with a sigh.

"What's the matter?" Gabe took her hand. "You haven't been your normal happy self this week."

"Do you think I'm judgmental?" The question popped out before Michelle could stop it.

Gabe's eyes widened. "Of course not. Why do you ask?"

"Not important," Michelle mumbled.

"Tell me." His thumb caressed her palm.

"Forget it." She pulled her hand back. "Let's talk about something happier."

"Hemorrhoids?" Gabe said, picking up on a nearby conversation.

"Definitely not." Michelle punched him in the side and he laughed.

"How about the moon? It's beautiful and the light makes your hair look like spun silk."

"Stop. You're going to make blush."

"I like to see you blush." Gabe lowered his voice. "All over."

"It seems like forever since we've been to the cabin," Michelle said with a sigh. "I miss it."

"I miss you." It was true. As much as Gabe enjoyed making love to her, it was simply being with her that he missed most of all.

Yet, the second her lips pressed tightly together, he knew it'd been the wrong thing to say.

"Our hanging out like this probably isn't a good idea." Michelle's gaze dropped to her hands.

Instead of responding, Gabe waited. He had a feeling he'd go wrong with either agreeing or disagreeing.

"It's too easy to forget that we're simply—" she lowered her voice to a mere whisper "—sleeping together."

"That's because it's not that simple. Making love is only part of what you and I share." Even though he wasn't sure this was the place to discuss such a sensitive matter, he was glad she'd brought up the subject. He'd been thinking a lot about their relationship recently. "I think we both made too big a deal about not dating. So what if neither one of us are looking for anything serious? Lots of people date without marriage in mind."

Michelle nodded and the tension in her shoulders appeared to ease. "That's true."

"What's wrong with simply having fun together?" His tone turned persuasive. "We could go to parties together. Have dinner, attend events like the upcoming groundbreaking celebration as a couple. What could it hurt?"

Michelle chewed on her lip and Gabe's stomach did a slow roll. He wasn't sure why it mattered so much to him that she agree. Except he wanted more. Not a lot more, just a little bit of a relationship. Yes, that was it.

"I suppose that makes sense." The doubtful look in her eyes told him she still wasn't fully convinced this was the right move. "We'd just have to keep in mind that the only thing between us is friendship."

"I won't have trouble doing that." He kept his tone light. "Will you?"

"Trust me, wanting more isn't going to be an issue with me."

It was exactly what he'd hoped she'd say, but her response left a sour taste in his mouth. How could she be so sure she wouldn't want more? He was a good guy. He had a lot of positive attributes.

Still, it didn't matter, because now he'd be able to enjoy her company without worrying about her expecting more from him than he was able to give.

## Chapter Fifteen

"Oh, my" was Michelle's first response when Gabe's truck approached the outside of the microbrewery in downtown Jackson. Even through the windows she could hear the sounds of music and laughter coming from inside.

The ground breaking of the veterans memorial garden project had been a whopping success. Now the celebration had moved downtown.

The lot just south of the building was already full. Seeing all the cars made her glad the committee had chosen this venue. The wine bar could have never accommodated this large a crowd.

Gabe dropped her off in front, then left to look for a parking space down the street. From the number of vehicles circling the brewery, he'd have to go a ways down the road to find an open spot.

He'd told her to go indoors and he'd find her. But Michelle didn't mind waiting outside. The temperature was still in the mid-seventies, unusually warm for a late-June night. The breeze was light and pleasant. All in all, it couldn't have been a better evening for a ground breaking and the party.

Even though Michelle was glad she'd come, part of her still wished she was back in bed with Gabe. Before the ground breaking they'd met at the cabin for a brief interlude.

She'd never known such a lover. While he was caring and sensitive, he was also the most adventurous. He'd mined depths to her that she didn't even know existed. Unfortunately he'd also brought emotions to the surface that she'd prefer to keep under wraps.

The door opened and Tripp stepped outside. A startled look of pleasure crossed his face. "You're finally here. I was beginning to think you and Gabe weren't coming." He glanced around. "Where is he?"

"Parking the truck."

His gaze slowly surveyed her formfitting blue dress. "I didn't get a chance to tell you at the ground breaking how lovely you look."

"Thank you." She noticed for the first time his gray dress pants and thin-striped shirt. "You look pretty spiffy yourself."

He grinned, showing a mouthful of perfect white teeth. "I aim to please."

Michelle realized that Tripp was a very attractive man, with his artfully disheveled blond hair and lean muscular body. While he might not make her heart beat even the tiniest bit faster, she could see why Adrianna was so enamored. "Where is she?"

His smile faded.

Her heart skipped a beat. "Is something wrong?"

"No." Tripp spoke quickly, as if wanting to reassure her. Or was it himself he wanted to convince?

His blue eyes, which normally sparkled with impish delight, were dark and troubled.

Michelle met his gaze. "Should I go find her?"

He shook his head. "The last I saw her she was talking to Betsy. Really, she's fine."

Betsy was Adrianna's best friend. If she was with her, then everything really was okay. Or would be soon.

"Why don't we sit down?" Michelle gestured to a decorative bench in front of the brewery. "I don't know why I wore these shoes. They always hurt my feet."

"Because they're stylish and make your legs look…incredible."

Michelle's lips twisted in a wry smile. "Oh, yeah, that was the reason."

"When you get inside take them off." Tripp sat down beside her.

"I'll think about it." Michelle already knew there was no way she was taking off her shoes at the party while the mayor was in attendance. "Tell me what's going on with you and Adrianna."

"Nothing." A shuttered look came over his face. "Like I've always said, we're just friends."

"Your choice? Her choice?"

"You're her friend," Tripp pointed out. "Next to Betsy, one of her best friends."

"True," Michelle acknowledged. "But that doesn't mean I'll tell her what you say. Anything you say to me stays right here. And that goes for what she's told me about you."

His eyes widened. "What has she said about me?"

Michelle couldn't help it. She laughed. "Didn't I just say I wouldn't tell you?"

"Give me a hint."

"Forget it." There was no way she'd betray any

of Adrianna's confidences. That was, of course, assuming that she knew any secrets. "The fact that you'd like to know her thoughts tells me that you're interested in her."

Tripp's eyes took on a distant look. "Even if Adrianna hadn't been a good friend of Gayle, we both have too much baggage to make a relationship work."

"So what do you want? A twenty-two-year-old who is just out of college and doesn't have a clue what life is really about?" Michelle gave a little laugh. "Good luck with that."

"What's between me and Adrianna would be complicated." He placed an arm lightly around her shoulder. "Now something between you and me—"

"Tripp, honey, there is no—"

"I had to park about a half mile down the road."

Michelle resisted the urge to groan aloud. From the look on Gabe's face he'd clearly misread the situation.

"You should have gotten here earlier." Tripp

pointed to his red BMW sports car parked out front.

Gabe ignored the car and glanced at Michelle. For a second she saw the man who kissed and caressed her only hours before. Then the look vanished, replaced by a polite mask. "Shall we go inside or do you prefer to stay with Tripp?"

Michelle refused to let this misunderstanding linger. Once they got inside there would be little privacy.

"Tripp, up." She put her hand on his back and he reluctantly stood. "Go inside and find Adrianna. Gabe and I will be in shortly."

"But—"

Before Tripp's protest could fully form, Michelle fixed her gaze on him.

"I'll see you later." He punched Gabe in the shoulder as he walked past.

Gabe rocked back on his heels.

"You two looked pretty cozy when I walked up," he said once the door closed behind Tripp.

Michelle exhaled a breath. At least they were

talking. Ed used to give her the silent treatment whenever he was upset.

"Looks can be deceiving," Michelle patted the spot next to her on the bench.

He shook his head. "I'm fine where I am."

But she didn't want him way over there. Michelle wanted him beside her. Where she could feel the heat from his body and reassure herself that all was okay between them.

"Please, Gabe, sit by me."

"Are you sure you don't want me to call Tripp back?" he asked when he sat down.

She punched him in the arm. Hard.

"Hey," he said. "What was that for?"

"You know very well who I want to be with, and he's sitting beside me now. Tripp is a friend. We were talking about Adrianna."

"He didn't look like he had your nurse-midwife on his mind when I walked up." Gabe took a finger and brushed a curl behind her ear. "It was you who appeared to be in his crosshairs."

"Tripp thinks a relationship with me would be

easier." Michelle gave a humorless laugh. "It's Adrianna he wants, but there's stuff between them."

"What kind of stuff?"

"Other than she was schoolgirl friends with his deceased wife, I'm not sure."

"What about Adrianna? Does she want him?"

"I think so, but I can't be positive. Adrianna is a very private person."

Gabe didn't press. "You're telling me he wasn't hitting on you?"

Michelle's initial impulse was to deny it. But honesty was important to both her and Gabe. She refused to bend the truth simply to ease the tension.

"He was headed toward that point," she acknowledged. "If I'd given him a green light, I think he'd have seized the opportunity and then regretted it. Like I said, I'm not who he really wants."

Gabe met her gaze. "You're who *I* want."

Michelle exhaled the breath that she didn't even

realize she'd been holding. "You're who I want, too. For now," she added.

He took her hand in his. "Thank you for being honest with me."

She smiled. "Honesty is as important to me as it is to you."

"We should go in," he said but made no move to get up. "Before I say to heck with the party and we head back to the cabin."

As much as Michelle wanted to do just that, life was about more than sex. Although right now, with Gabe so close and desire coursing through her blood like a hot stream of lava, she couldn't remember why.

She pushed to her feet and held out a hand to him.

Instead of rising as she expected, he tugged her down and kissed her softly on the lips.

It was gentle and sweet and brought emotions and a hope she'd kept under tight control from rushing to the surface.

He stood and slipped her hand through the crook of his arm. "Now I'm ready."

Just before they reached the front door, she reached up and wiped off a smudge from the corner of his lip.

He cocked his head.

"Lipstick," she explained and he smiled.

Gabe opened the large oak door with the beveled glass and stepped back to let her enter.

"There's sure a lot of people here," she whispered.

"They wouldn't have even noticed if we didn't show," Gabe responded in an equally low tone.

"Don't be too sure." Michelle smiled as Mary Karen and Travis swept through the crowd to greet them.

"I asked Tripp and Adrianna if you were coming and they assured me that you were." Mary Karen looked lovely in a periwinkle-blue cashmere sweater and silky skirt.

"I told them you better show up." Travis reached out to shake Gabe's hand and brushed a kiss across Michelle's cheek. "We have enough food to feed an army."

Travis was in charge of the committee arranging the food and drink for the celebration.

"We wouldn't have missed it," Gabe said.

*We.*

Michelle caught the look Mary Karen slanted her husband. The next time she saw the couple she knew she'd be interrogated within an inch of her life.

But she wasn't going to worry about that now. Tonight she was going to enjoy being part of a couple.

"The food and drinks are all along the bar, as well as any you can grab from passing waiters," Mary Karen explained. "Speaking of which—"

She reached out and plucked a flute of champagne from a passing waiter, then gestured for them to have a glass.

Gabe took two, handing one to Michelle, then keeping one for himself. Travis shook his head when the waiter glanced questioningly at him.

"One of us has to keep a clear head," Travis said, good-naturedly shooting his wife a wink.

"He's being the adult." Mary Karen smiled up at her husband. "I'm not."

"I'm on call tonight." Travis smiled and slipped an arm around his wife's shoulder, giving it an affectionate squeeze.

"How did that happen?" Michelle asked. "I thought you'd taken the night off."

"Actually, I'm backup. Tim Duggan was supposed to be, but he broke his leg this afternoon."

"Oh, no," Michelle said. "I'm sorry to hear it. I hope you don't get called out."

"That makes two of us." Travis smiled, then gestured to the crowded room. "Enjoy."

Gabe gripped her arm more tightly as they plunged forward into the sea of people. But once they began to circulate, Michelle relaxed. Most in attendance were friends. Or if they weren't, they were fond acquaintances.

Even though Gabe didn't know quite as many people as she did, she was surprised by how many greeted him by name. For those he didn't know, it made Michelle feel good to introduce him. She felt proud to be at his side.

It had been a while since she'd attended a party with a man. When someone hurrying through the crowd got too close, Gabe pulled her close and protected her with his body. When her feet began to hurt too much, she held on to him while slipping off her shoes. She found herself enjoying the party far more than she would have alone.

They ran across Adrianna and Tripp when they ventured outside to the back patio. The two were sitting on a glider, not as close as you'd expect for a couple, but close enough that you could tell at a glance they weren't simply casual acquaintances.

"Looks like they're having a serious discussion," Gabe said in a low tone.

"If we don't say hello now, with all the people we might not see them again tonight," Michelle said.

Gabe shrugged. "Up to you."

She took his arm. "Let's do it."

As they stopped before the couple, Gabe moved his arm around her waist. Almost as if he wanted to make sure Tripp understood she was here with him and he'd be the one taking her home.

From the flicker in Tripp's eyes, he'd gotten the message loud and clear.

"We didn't want to interrupt," Michelle began then stopped realizing, like Gabe, she'd made them a couple with her "we." "But I saw you and—"

"—we wanted to say hello," Gabe filled in the gap when she faltered.

Adrianna's eyes were red-rimmed. If you looked closely, it was apparent she'd been crying. Michelle didn't know what to say. She'd never seen the nurse-midwife cry. No matter how sad the situation.

Yet, she'd cried tonight. At a party.

What had Tripp said to her?

Michelle shot him a glare, but there was only concern, not guilt, in his eyes. She shifted her attention to her friend, unsure how to proceed.

Even though she and Adrianna had worked together for over two years, other than her academic achievements, Michelle knew very little about Adrianna's private life. She certainly had no knowledge of what had happened that had caused her to distrust men.

"You should try the champagne." Michelle lifted her half empty flute. "It's the best I've ever tasted."

"Want some?" Tripp asked.

Adrianna shrugged. "I suppose so."

Tripp jumped up. "I'll run some down."

"I'll go with you," Gabe said, then turned to Michelle. "We won't be long."

"Take your time." Michelle took the space Tripp had vacated and dropped her shoes to the concrete. "Adrianna and I will keep each other company."

"What's with the no shoes?" Adrianna asked.

"I loved the looks of these, but they pinch my toes something terrible." Michelle glanced at

Adrianna's four-inch stylish stilettos. "I don't know how you can walk in those."

For the first time since they'd interrupted, Adrianna smiled and flexed her foot. "They're actually quite comfortable."

"Perhaps I need to look at a different brand," Michelle said doubtfully.

"We don't need to talk around it." Adrianna shifted in her seat to face Michelle. "I received a text and I got upset and cried. It was something personal and had nothing to do with Tripp."

Adrianna must have seen the skepticism in Michelle's eyes because she smiled. "Truly. And I feel badly, because he doesn't know what to do. But there's nothing I expect from him."

"That's kind of an odd thing to say."

"That I don't expect anything from him? Not so odd." Adrianna brushed a piece of chestnut hair back from her face. "I've learned not to expect much from anyone."

Michelle knew Adrianna didn't mean to be

hurtful, but she wondered if that meant Adrianna didn't trust *her*. "I hope that doesn't include me."

"I know you'd do your best to always stand by me."

It wasn't a ringing endorsement but Michelle had the feeling it was the best she was going to get. "Is there anything I can do?"

Adrianna's emerald eyes gave nothing away. "Just don't blame Tripp. He's a good friend."

"He is?"

"But not as good of a friend as Gabe is to you." The smile that appeared on Adrianna's lips reached her eyes. "Something is going on between you two."

"I like Gabe," Michelle said, not sure how much to divulge. "And I think he likes me."

"There's no *think* about it," a deep voice interrupted.

Michelle wanted to sink through the concrete as she looked up into Gabe's smiling face.

If there was a way that she could figure out how to do it, she'd be six feet under. Dear God, he must think he was hanging out with some high school girl, gossiping with her friends about boys.

"Ah, there's not?" she asked when the silence became uncomfortable.

"No," he leaned down and kissed her full on the mouth in front of everyone. "I *do* like you. Very much."

## Chapter Sixteen

"You realize I'm not going to be able to live that kiss down," Michelle said to Gabe as he pulled into their driveway.

"That little peck on the lips?" His mouth turned upward in full smirk.

"It may have started out that way." Michelle resisted the urge to touch her lips. "That's not how it ended."

"And whose fault was that?" he teased.

Okay, so perhaps she'd gotten a little carried away. But he'd certainly gone along with her... exuberance. "I guess mine."

"I think we both were really into it."

"Did you see Adrianna's eyes?" Michelle chuckled. "Certainly made her forget her troubles for a few seconds."

Gabe shut off the truck and shifted in his seat to face her. "What's up with her?"

"I honestly don't know." She slowly unbuckled her seat belt. "But Adrianna is a strong woman with a lot of supportive friends. I told her I'll always be there for her. I got the feeling she didn't believe me."

He reached over and cupped the back of her neck with his hand. "Sounds like she was disappointed in the past by someone she trusted. Those wounds take a long time to heal."

The sensuous touch of his stroking fingers made it difficult for Michelle to think. "Has that ever happened to you?"

Instead of just tossing off some answer, Gabe's fingers stilled. "I was disappointed when Shannon walked away from Finley and me, but I didn't feel betrayed. She'd made it clear from the time she found out she was pregnant that she didn't want…to be a mother."

Even though Gabe had only said his girlfriend hadn't wanted to be a *mother,* Michelle could read between the lines. "Did she ever consider having an abortion?"

"She may have briefly considered that option." Gabe appeared to choose his words carefully. "But I believe she's always been glad she continued the pregnancy."

"Usually once I put the baby in a mother's arms—" Michelle's voice grew thick with emotion "—she knows she's made the right decision."

"Shannon never did warm to Finley." Gabe fixed his gaze over her shoulder as if embarrassed by the admission. "By the time she gave birth, she'd pretty much made the decision to leave."

Michelle softened her tone. "How long did she stick around?"

"Two months." Gabe took a breath, then let it out slowly. "She gave it eight weeks."

"Does she keep in contact with Finley?"

"Not at all."

Michelle thought of her own mother. Even though a thousand miles now separated them, her mom called at least once a week. She couldn't imagine not having her. Never having her.

Finley had never known a mother's love. Michelle's heart gave a ping. "How does Finley feel about that?"

"It hurts her. She says it's okay, that she has her grandma. But it's not the same." Gabe's lips twisted. "I've tried to sit down and talk with her about it, but that only seems to make it worse."

"She probably feels rejected," Michelle murmured. His daughter's face, with those beautiful eyes and sensitive features, flashed before Michelle. She wondered if Shannon truly realized what she'd given up.

"Enough about that." Gabe's tone made it clear the subject was closed. His gaze met hers. "What about you? Anyone ever let you down?"

There were dozens of things Michelle could

have said that would have made it seem like she was honestly answering his question without actually doing so. But she wanted to be as honest with him as he'd been with her. "Ed."

"Your ex?"

She nodded. "I thought he wanted a wife, a true partner. I hoped we could be a family." The old hurt welled inside her, but she realized it didn't sting quite so much anymore. "He had two daughters about Finley's age—Chrissy and Ann. It was like the three of them had their own little club, one I wasn't allowed to join. I tried many times to talk with Ed about it, but he couldn't see why I cared. He kept telling me I should be glad to not be involved in his daughters' lives. But I always felt like I was on the outside looking in."

Not only had Michelle shared more than she'd meant to, but the words also kept coming. Like a large boulder on a downhill slide, she couldn't seem to stop. She told Gabe everything, including how the girls had treated her with such disrespect and how Ed didn't do a thing to stop it.

Gabe's brows drew together as her voice began to shake. He took her hand and murmured soothing words of reassurance until she'd said it all. The only part she left out was her resolve never to marry a man with a teenager.

"Unimaginable." He brought her hand to his lips. "But his loss is my gain."

The first of the week came and went with Gabe only seeing Michelle in passing. They'd wave or stop to talk in the driveway for a second. But it seemed either she had some place to be or he did.

By Thursday, missing her had grown to an acute ache. It wasn't only the lovemaking that Gabe missed, but also talking to her for more than two or three minutes at a time. He understood that her career was a demanding one. Lately he'd seen her car pull into the garage at all hours of the night.

*If we lived in the same house, I'd be there for her when she got home,* Gabe thought as he studied the blueprints spread out on a sheet of plywood held up by two sawhorses.

The thought should have shocked him, but instead it felt right. He loved Michelle. He wasn't sure when like had turned to love, but it didn't matter. They should be together.

Because of Finley, he could never live with Michelle without being married. And although Michelle appeared to like Finley well enough, he needed to be certain of her feelings for his daughter.

He and Finley were a package deal. Any woman he married would have to love his daughter.

*Marriage.*

Just thinking of the word brought him up short. What happened to his plans of focusing on his career and Finley's acclimation to Jackson Hole before even dating? Michelle. She was what happened. Somehow without his realizing how it had happened, she'd found a place in his heart.

"Is there a problem with those prints?"

Gabe jerked his head up and found Joel standing beside him, a knowing smile on his lips.

"They look good." Gabe gestured with his head to the blueprints. "I was just thinking about the time frame for this project."

"The time frame, huh?" Joel rubbed his chin. "Sure you weren't thinking about a certain lady doctor instead?"

Gabe was deciding on the best response when the sound of a car climbing the steep mountain road drew both their attention. The red van that pulled up next to the assortment of work vehicles was a familiar one.

A broad smile split Joel's face. "Looks like the family decided to pay me a visit."

Kate got out of the vehicle, looking stylish in bright yellow pants and a shirt with every color under the sun. She waved before opening the side door of the van and unbuckling Chloe.

The little girl immediately hopped out and ran straight for her dad. She was three or four years younger than Finley, still at that gawky age where they seemed to be all arms and legs and big teeth. Yet the girl reminded Gabe of her lovely mother and Gabe had no doubt Chloe would one day be as beautiful.

"Daddy, Daddy." Chloe ran to Joel, wrapping her arms around him as if it had been months since she'd last seen him instead of a few hours. "We brought you a picnic lunch. I helped Mommy make the potato salad."

Joel returned his daughter's hug and planted a kiss on the top of her black silky hair. "Then I'll definitely have an extra helping."

"Keep in mind this is a new recipe," Kate joked, approaching them with a car seat swinging from one hand. "Lexi gave it to me but…no promises."

"Let me help you with this." Joel gently removed the infant carrier from her hand. "Are you supposed to be doing all this heavy lifting?"

"Michelle took me off all restrictions when I saw her last week. Remember?" Kate brushed a piece of dark hair back from her face and turned to Gabe. "I brought enough for you, too. If you don't already have plans, that is."

"I don't think Gabe received any texts today," Joel said with a chuckle.

Kate cocked her head.

"Inside joke." Gabe kept his tone matter-of-fact. "If you don't think I'd be in the way, I'd love to join you."

Gabe settled his gaze on Joel's family. His boss was a lucky man. Joel had a woman he loved and his kids had both a father and a mother.

The lunch hour went quickly, with Gabe taking a turn holding baby Sam. He gazed down at the tiny bundle. "I remember when Finley was this age."

"Eight weeks old tomorrow." Kate's lips lifted in a proud smile. "And he slept five hours last night."

"They grow up quickly." Joel cast a fond smile in his daughter's direction. "I swear Chloe's grown at least three inches since last year."

"Oh, Dad." Chloe's face reddened with embarrassment.

Kate pulled her daughter close. "Daddies love to tease. That's just how they are."

Then suddenly it was time for them to leave. Joel walked his family to the van, helping Kate secure the baby and Chloe in their car seats. Gabe went back to studying the blueprints while Joel gave his wife a goodbye kiss.

When Joel sauntered back in Gabe's direction, he was whistling.

"That was nice of Kate to bring lunch," Gabe commented.

"Once she goes back to her practice, that's not going to happen too often," Joel said with a rueful smile. "So I'm enjoying it now."

Kate was a pediatrician in Jackson and had a thriving practice. Although she was Chloe's biological mother, she'd given her daughter up for adoption when she was beginning medical school. She and Joel had connected after his first wife had died. That was all Gabe knew for sure, although he'd heard bits and pieces of rumors, most of which he ignored.

"Do you have a sitter lined up?"

"The young woman who watches Chloe in the summer has agreed to care for Sam, too." Joel's gaze turned thoughtful. "We're both committed to making our home life our priority. Kate has been talking to the other doctors in her practice about ways to cut back her hours."

"Can I ask you a personal question?"

"You can ask." Joel grinned. "Won't guarantee I'll answer."

"Did Chloe have any trouble accepting Kate into her life? Or does she still blame her for giving her up?"

Joel's brows slammed together like two dark thunderclouds.

"I'm just looking for some tips," Gabe said hurriedly, wanting to make sure Joel understood that he wasn't dissing his wife. "Finley won't even discuss her mother with me. It makes me wonder if she could ever accept a new woman in my life."

The tension on Joel's face eased. "Those are two very different questions. From the time Chloe was old enough to understand, Amy and I made sure she knew that adoption was a caring choice. That her birth mother had loved her so much that she picked Amy and me to be her mommy and daddy. It was difficult when she found out Kate was her mother. But she did pretty well considering it was quite a shock. The counselor we hired also helped."

"I took Finley to a counselor several years back, but she wouldn't say a word." Gabe shook his head. "Just sat there with her arms crossed. After that she stopped saying how much she hated her mother. But I know she still does."

"Sometimes it just takes the right person." Joel shrugged. "Chloe really liked Dr. Allman."

"I suppose it's too much to hope that Finley will simply outgrow these feelings...."

"What do you think?"

"You're right." Gabe expelled a breath and forced his gaze back on the blueprint.

"What's this about a new woman in your life?" Joel's gaze turned speculative. "I assume you're referring to Michelle."

"Michelle is a wonderful woman and I enjoy her company." Gabe paused, unsure how much to share. "I'm not certain yet if it will develop into more. Finley is a big factor."

"How do the two of them get along?"

"Good." Gabe thought of how Michelle had trusted Finley to watch Sasha, how easily she'd adapted when Finley had ridden with them to Travis and Mary Karen's party. "Really good, in fact."

"So you have no reason to think there might be a problem there?"

Gabe thought for a moment and shook his head. "No, but they haven't spent that much time together either."

"Well, I guess you'll just have to figure out a way to make that happen."

Gabe rubbed his chin. "I guess I will."

One of the framers called to Joel.

"I'll be right there," Joel told the guy, then turned back to Gabe. "By the way, I'm heading to Montana tomorrow afternoon to check out the operations there. I'd like you to come with me. We'll be back Saturday night."

Gabe had been hoping for this opportunity, but he hadn't thought far enough ahead to realize that because of the distance, he'd be gone overnight. "I'll need to find someone to watch Finley."

"I'd volunteer Kate, but she's supervising a lock-in for the upper-grade elementary students at the church tomorrow night."

"I'll ask Lexi if Finley can stay over," Gabe murmured. "They spend so much time at one house or the other it shouldn't be too much of an imposition."

"Or," Joel suggested, a twinkle in his eyes, "if that doesn't work out, there's always your neighbor."

## Chapter Seventeen

Once Gabe knew he'd be leaving town the next day, the last thing he felt like doing was attending the Taste of Jackson Hole at Teton Village.

But Stone Craft Builders fully supported the popular three-day Jackson Hole wine auction. The events centered around this auction benefited the Grand Teton Music Festival which was one of the nation's leading music festivals. No matter how tired he was, he needed to be there.

He thought about asking Michelle if she was going, but when he got home, her house was dark.

Joel had told him the dress was casual, so Gabe changed into a pair of khakis and a plaid shirt.

"Why can't I go with you?" Finley whined.

"It's not for…teenagers." Gabe stopped himself just in time from saying *children,* a word guaranteed to inflame any thirteen-year-old. "If I had the option, I'd stay home with you this evening."

"It's supposed to be supercool." Finley leaned forward from her position on the sofa. "They have all these chefs and restaurants making their most popular foods to go with the wines."

Gabe grinned. "Sounds like you know more about it than I do."

"They were talking about it on the radio today," Finley informed him. "The restaurant is at the top of Rendezvous Mountain. You have to ride a gondola to get there. I've never ridden a gondola up a mountain."

Suddenly her intense interest in the event made sense. It wasn't the food and wine that interested his daughter as much as the gondola ride.

"How about next week you and I take Addie

to dinner at the Couloir Restaurant at the top of the mountain as a thank-you for allowing you to spend the night tomorrow?"

"That'd be awesome." Finley's eyes sparkled. "Having her along will be a lot more fun than just you and me."

"Gee, thanks."

Finley giggled. "You know what I mean. We talk about things that don't really interest you."

"That's fine," Gabe said with melodramatic flare. "I can be the third wheel."

"You could bring Michelle," Finley surprised him by suggesting. "If you wanted to, that is."

"I'll keep that option in mind." Gabe suddenly wondered if he'd worried over nothing. It sounded as if his daughter had already accepted Michelle being in his life.

Unless, of course, that was only his own wishful thinking.

Michelle left the office early to attend the premier wine tasting which opened the Jackson Hole

Wine Auction. She'd never attended before, but Mitzi Sanchez, one of Kate's friends and an orthopedic surgeon in town, had asked Michelle to come with her.

She didn't know Mitzi well but quickly found the beautiful Latina had a sense of humor in sync with her own. And they both had an interest in the lecture by a noted wine critic on what elements comprise a great wine.

After the presentation and tasting, the two women decided it was time for food. With her bright blue eyes and brown hair streaked the color of peanut butter, her companion drew men's gazes wherever they walked. Kate laughingly described her friend as a chameleon who could change her look and personality to fit any situation.

Today, Mitzi had gone with the bohemian look. While most women, including Michelle, had opted for a pair of dress pants topped with a summer sweater, Mitzi wore a dress.

And not just any dress, but a tiered maxi with

boots. The crazy thing was she looked adorable. Not like a well-respected member of the Jackson medical community, but rather a funky fashionista. Her associate, Benedict Campbell, certainly seemed to think so. The wealthy bachelor had spirited Mitzi away, ostensibly to talk about some case.

Michelle had heard through the grapevine that the two had a love-hate relationship.

"Are you here by yourself?"

Michelle whirled, recognizing the familiar deep voice. "Gabe."

Dressed casually in khakis and a plaid shirt, Gabe fit right in with the casual crowd. It felt like days since they'd had a chance to talk and even longer since they'd…

"Is that a croquette on your plate, Dr. Kerns?"

Michelle glanced down. She couldn't stop from smiling. "Why, yes, I believe it is."

"I bet it's made with Rofumo cheese." Gabe somehow managed to keep a straight face. "In case you're not aware, Rofumo is a semisoft cheese smoked over hickory wood."

"You don't say." Michelle grinned. "You're quite the gourmet, Mr. Davis."

Gabe lowered his voice. "It's the only item I recognize. I feel like I'm back at Lexi's buffet."

"You have to admit, everything is good."

He met her gaze, then lowered his, taking in her red V-necked sweater, letting his gaze linger. "Everything is delicious."

"Are you talking about the food?"

"Do you want me to be talking about the food?" He glanced around. "And you never answered my question. Are you here with anyone?"

Michelle turned in the direction where she'd last seen her companion. "I'm with—"

She paused and blinked. Mitzi and Benedict were no longer where she'd last seen them. In fact, they were nowhere in sight. "I came with Mitzi Sanchez. But I believe she's been hijacked by Ben Campbell."

"Then I'd like permission to hijack you."

"Because you asked so nicely—" Michelle slipped her hand through his arm "—I say yes."

"Have you had a chance to check out the silent auction?" he asked.

"Not yet."

They picked up a few more food items and tried some samples of wine, then moved to the area where the silent auction items were displayed. It was there they ran across Mitzi and Ben.

"I'm so sorry." Mitzi hurried up to Michelle. "Ben and I started talking about this upcoming surgical case—"

"No worries," Michelle reassured her, then introduced Gabe. There was an instant bond between him and Mitzi when she heard of his connection with the Dennes family.

"Kate and I go way back," Mitzi gushed. "She's the reason I chose to practice in Jackson Hole."

"And to have the opportunity to work with me," Ben interjected.

"Forgive him. He can't help it." Mitzi rolled her eyes. "The man has an ego the size of Grand Teton."

Michelle hid a laugh. Ben didn't seem amused by the comparison to the highest mountain in the Tetons.

"If you don't mind—" Gabe's hand remained on her arm "—I told Michelle I'd take her home."

"You don't have to do that," Mitzi said, then slanted a sideways glance at Ben. "Of course, that would mean we could go back to the office and further discuss the case."

Ben seemed up for the idea. After chatting for several minutes, the two sauntered off.

"What was that about?" Michelle asked when they were out of earshot. "You never asked if you could take me home."

"Of course not." Gabe grinned. "This is a hijacking. And I'm not taking you home. I'm taking you to the cabin."

Michelle relaxed against Gabe's warm flesh, trying to remember the last time she'd felt this happy. She loved the way he held and kissed her. But she also loved simply being with him.

He nuzzled her neck. "And to think I dreaded this evening."

She snuggled deeper into the crook of his arm, wishing they didn't have to go home. Wishing the night would never end. Wishing she and Gabe could be together forever.

The thought brought her up short. She tensed and sat up in the bed just as his cell phone rang.

He tugged on her arm. "Come back here."

Her heart had begun to pound. "You better answer. It might be Finley."

"It's not. She set her ringtone on my phone to the *Hunger Games* bird call."

Michelle reached over him, the sheet dropping to her waist. She grabbed the phone and glanced at the readout just as his hand closed over her breast, his thumb moving to the sensitive nipple. She inhaled sharply as his nail scraped across the tip and heat flowed straight to her core. "It's—it's Lexi."

He lifted his head, his eyes dark and smoldering. "I'm busy."

Michelle slipped back from his reach. "You have to talk to her. I know Lex. She'll keep calling until she reaches you."

Giving a grunt of disgust, he took the phone from her fingers and caught the call just before it went to voice mail. "Hey, Lex. What's up?"

Michelle could tell the news wasn't good by the look on his face. But all he kept saying was that he understood and everything would be fine. After thanking her for calling, he hung up.

He plopped back against the pillow and ran his fingers through his hair. "Now what am I going to do?"

"What's the matter?" Michelle asked. "Can I help?"

He shifted to his side to face her. "Are you serious?"

The sudden gleam in his eyes should have warned her.

"Of course," she said.

"Well, tomorrow I have to go to Montana and..."

* * *

Michelle realized later that a woman would agree to almost anything while in bed with a handsome man. Last night in the dim light of the cabin bedroom, with Gabe's arms around her, she'd found herself agreeing to watch Finley Friday night and all day Saturday while Gabe went out of town for work.

Apparently the plans he'd made for Finley to stay at Lexi's house had fallen through when Addie came down with the crud Gabe had last week. Michelle had made it clear to Gabe that she could get called out to the hospital at any time. He told her that was fine, he just didn't want Finley home alone overnight.

*It's only for one night,* Michelle told herself when the knock sounded.

Gabe stood on her front stoop, his daughter at his side.

"I told Dad I'd be fine staying by myself," Finley said in lieu of greeting. "But he said no way."

Finley didn't look happy about the decision, but

she and Gabe must have been down this road before because he didn't react.

"Thank you." To Michelle's surprise, after giving Finley a quick hug, Gabe turned to her and kissed her on the cheek. "Have fun. I'll be back sometime tomorrow evening."

The wariness on the girl's face disappeared when Sasha nosed in beside Michelle, wagging her tail. "Hey, Sasha."

"I told her you were coming." Michelle opened the door wide and motioned Finley inside. "She's been so excited. Are you hungry?"

"I already ate," Finley said, belatedly adding, "but thank you for offering."

"Then how about dessert?" Michelle took Finley's bag from her hands, leaving the girl free to pet Sasha, who was now shimmying on her belly toward her. "I thought we could go to Hill of Beans. They have blackberry cobbler on Fridays. Unless you're too full?"

Sasha had now rolled on her back. Finley looked up, but continued to scratch the retriever's belly. A smile lifted her lips. "The way I see it, there's always room for cobbler."

Michelle couldn't explain the sense of relief that flooded her. She found herself wanting to whistle as she reached for her keys. "I guess that leaves one last decision. Do we split or get our own?"

While meeting Joel's crew in Montana and touring their current job sites had been invaluable in better understanding the entire scope of Stone Craft's operations, by the time they pulled into Jackson and Gabe retrieved his pickup, he was eager to get home.

Even though he'd tried to call Finley and Michelle several times while he was gone. There had been no landline on the building sites. The cell reception in the mountainous area had been spotty at best and he'd never reached them.

Gabe told himself everything was fine. He'd made sure before he dropped her off that Finley understood she needed to be on her best behavior.

He wasn't sure what he'd find when he drove up, but when he saw Finley and Michelle in the driveway, shooting hoops, his lips widened into a grin. He pulled into the garage, then quickly hopped out and joined them.

"That was *R*," Finley called out to Michelle.

"Are you sure?" Michelle argued. "I think I was only at *O*."

"Hey, Dad." Finley pulled the ball close to her chest and sauntered over to him, giving him a one-armed hug. "Welcome back."

Michelle was only steps behind. "Was it a good trip?"

"It was." Gabe glanced from the woman to the girl, liking the smiles on their faces and their ease with each other. "I was glad I went, but it's good to be back."

"Did you know Michelle used to play college ball?" Finley asked him, clearly impressed.

"I think she mentioned that to me," he said with a smile.

"She told me I have potential." Finley glanced at Michelle and she nodded. "She offered to help me with my jump shot."

"That's nice of you," Gabe said to Michelle. Warmth rose inside him. He'd hoped the two would get along when they were alone, but never had he imagined this easy camaraderie.

"We had fun," Michelle said with a decisive nod.

"We went to Hill of Beans last night and got vanilla bean ice cream *and* whipped cream on top of the blueberry cobbler. We were such pigs," Finley said with a happy smile.

"Pigs, huh?" Gabe shifted his gaze from his lanky daughter to Michelle's voluptuous figure without an ounce of visible fat. "Guess it's a good thing you're working off all those calories."

"What time is it?" Finley asked abruptly.

"Almost eight."

"I'm going to run inside and call Addie real

quick. I want to see if she's feeling better and will be in church tomorrow."

When Finley handed him the basketball, Gabe expected her to immediately take off for the house. Instead she turned to Michelle.

"Thank you for letting me stay with you." Finley followed up the polite words with a quick hug. "I had an awesome time."

Without another word, the girl headed inside.

Gabe stared at Michelle. "Wow, I never imagined things would go so well."

"It surprised me, too," Michelle looked positively misty-eyed. "She's a great kid."

With those four words, suddenly all was right in Gabe's world.

"What's the matter?" she asked.

Michelle wore biker shorts and a faded T. A strand of hair had pulled loose from her ponytail. There was a smudge of dirt on one cheek. He'd never seen her look more beautiful or loved her more. He took a step closer. "I missed you."

Her bright smile wobbled. "Ditto."

Without taking his eyes off her, Gabe flung the ball on the lawn. It rolled for a few feet, then stopped. With his hands finally free, he did what he'd wanted to do since he'd driven up and seen her in the driveway in those cute black shorts and T-shirt showing all that skin. He grabbed her hand and tugged her close.

She resisted, but only a little.

"Someone will see," she murmured, wrapping her arms around his neck.

"Let them," he growled. "I can't go another second without kissing you."

Michelle lifted her face to his. "In that case…"

When her body molded against him, it was as if she was the other half he needed to make him whole.

He settled his hands on her hips, trying to bring her even closer. "Thank you."

"I told you," she whispered, sliding her fingers into his hair, "Finley was no trouble."

"No. Thank you for being you." Gabe's eyes met hers. "I was beginning to think I'd never find you."

His mouth closed over hers and suddenly close wasn't close enough. Michelle must have felt the same way because she pressed her body even tighter against him and opened her mouth to his probing tongue.

"Dad."

His daughter's voice was like a splash of cold water.

Michelle stiffened and jerked away.

Gabe turned, grateful the increasing darkness hid the tightness of his jeans.

Finley's face gave nothing away. "Addie's parents want to know what we're doing for the fourth."

"Uh, tell them I'll call them tomorrow if I don't see them in church."

Finley's gaze shifted from him to Michelle. "Okay."

She disappeared back into the house, pulling the door shut behind her.

"She saw us, you know." Michelle sounded concerned.

"It's for the best." Gabe realized it was past time he talked with his daughter about his feelings for Michelle. "I want her to know that you're important to me. That I care about you. That I—"

Michelle's fingers closed over his lips, stopping his words. "We're friends."

"We're more than friends."

Her lips curved upward. "Perhaps."

"There's no perhaps about it," Gabe insisted stubbornly.

"It's important we take this slow. There's a lot at stake for both of us."

"Tell me what you're really saying."

"We take it as slow as it needs to go. Until you're sure." Her eyes were clear and solemn. "Until I'm sure. That means no declarations of feelings and no promises."

"I don't like it."

"I'm not sure I do either." She kissed him on the mouth. "But for now it's the wisest course to take."

## *Chapter Eighteen*

Gabe couldn't remember what he'd done last year on the Fourth of July, but this year's celebration was off to a great start. Michelle had accompanied him and Finley to the pancake breakfast in Town Square put on by the Jaycees every year. She'd even made it through much of the parade that followed before getting called to the hospital.

But that was almost two hours ago. Apparently things in labor and delivery were moving slower than she'd anticipated. She'd promised to meet them once the baby made its appearance at Alpine Field for Music in the Hole, an annual event put on by the Grand Teton Music Festival.

Even though Finley had initially acted put out that Michelle would be coming with them, the two had gotten along great all morning. When Michelle had asked him why he was smiling, he'd told her because it was such a beautiful day. The truth was, seeing her and Finley having fun together was a dream come true.

"I'd hate to be a doctor." Finley appeared irritated by the fact that Michelle wasn't yet back. "Michelle never has any free time."

"There are things she has to give up," Gabe admitted, reflecting on everything Michelle had told him about her career. "But I know she finds it very rewarding."

"I hope that baby doesn't take all day to get born." Finley cast a pointed glance at the picnic basket in her father's hand. "Otherwise we're going to be stuck with a ton of food."

Gabe shot her a wink. "Maybe I can invite my friends over for a party."

"Or maybe—" Finley's eyes took on a teasing glint "—I can invite *my* friends over for a party. After all, Michelle and I did make most of the food."

"Yeah, what did you spend, like a whole day cooking and baking?"

"Just one evening, Dad." Finley rolled her eyes, but there was a smile on her lips. "Fried chicken—"

"Gabe Davis." A tall woman with dark hair stepped in front of him, an astonished look on her face. "I haven't seen you in years."

It took Gabe a second. He did know her. Something about her smile tripped his memory. "Lisa Sindelar?"

"Lisa Delperding now." A little laugh escaped her bright red lips. Her smile faded when she saw Finley.

Finley shifted from one foot to the other, a tentative smile on her lips. She didn't know the woman. Couldn't have known her. Gabe's acquaintance with the brunette went back to a time before she was born.

"This is my daughter, Finley." Gabe placed a hand on his daughter's shoulder before completing the introductions.

Lisa's curious gaze turned sharp and assessing. "I see Shannon in her eyes."

Beneath his hand, Gabe felt Finley's shoulder stiffen. He should have known Lisa would bring up Shannon. The two had been on the same cheerleading squad and good friends.

"Do you know my mother?" Finley surprised him by asking.

Gabe couldn't believe Finley was pursuing the conversation. Normally she turned and hightailed it the other way whenever her mother was mentioned.

Lisa's smile broadened as if she'd been pulling up to a red light that had suddenly turned green. "I've known Shannon for years. We ran around together in high school. We even pledged the same sorority in college."

Finley's smile froze on her face. She was old enough to realize that Shannon's sorority pledge had come mere months after leaving her.

"I wasn't aware you'd moved to Jackson Hole," Gabe said when the silence lengthened.

"We still live back in Philly." Lisa appeared oblivious to the tension in the air. "I'm here with my family on vacation. That's my husband, Steven, over there with our two little ones."

Gabe glanced in the direction that Lisa indicated and lifted a hand in greeting to the blond man holding the hands of a preschool boy and a baby wearing a bright pink hat in his arms.

"Rose is the same age as Abby, Doug and Shannon's little one." A smile lifted Lisa's lips. "You should see how Shannon dotes on that baby. It's so sweet."

"I'll find us a spot to sit." Finley jerked from Gabe's light grasp and stalked away without another word.

Normally he'd call her back, make her say a proper goodbye to an adult she'd just met. But

Gabe had seen the stricken look on his daughter's face. She'd been only seconds away from either lashing out or bursting into tears.

"Did you have to say that?" Gabe saw no need to couch his own irritation behind a mask of civility.

"Say what?" For a second the woman looked puzzled. Until her gaze settled on Finley's back. She brought her fingers to her lips. "Oh, I didn't think—"

"That's right," Gabe snapped, "you didn't think. Shannon doesn't think about Finley's feelings either."

With great effort, Gabe reined in his temper. It wasn't fair to take out his frustrations about Shannon's lack of interest in Finley on Lisa.

"I hope you enjoy your stay in Jackson Hole." Without waiting for a reply, Gabe turned and hurried off to catch up with Finley.

Michelle texted Gabe as soon as she got to Alpine Field. With all the noise from the music and the crowd, she doubted he'd hear a cell phone ring.

He responded immediately with his location. Smiling, she began weaving her way through the blankets and lawn chairs to a point just south of a large red-and-white striped tent. It took a bit longer than she'd anticipated because she kept running into people she knew.

As she chatted and laughed, Michelle realized that life didn't get much better. The sun shone bright overhead. The sky was a vivid blue. And she was going to spend the day with Gabe and Finley.

She'd discovered she enjoyed being with Gabe *and* his daughter. She and Finley had even spent some fun moments together since the girl had caught her and Gabe kissing. Not like Ed's daughters who'd immediately brought out their claws when they'd realized her and Ed's relationship was getting serious.

Michelle stopped to dutifully admire a baby she'd delivered three months ago. But even as she laughed and joked with the parents, her mind was miles away. Having Finley for a stepdaughter no longer seemed so abhorrent. In fact, she kind of liked the idea.

Her phone buzzed. She glanced down.

R U lost?

"Baby on the way?" the infant's father asked.

"Actually, the friend I'm meeting is concerned I lost my way." Michelle slipped the phone back in her pocket, said her goodbyes and started walking, determined not to get waylaid again.

She found Gabe and Finley just where Gabe had said they would be. They'd brought not only a blanket but also three lawn chairs. Michelle guessed the empty one to Gabe's right was for her.

It didn't register at first that Gabe and Finley weren't talking. Music from the bandstand filled the air. It only figured they'd be listening to that.

"Hey, guys." Michelle smiled as she walked up. "I'm here."

"Finally," Finley muttered and Gabe shot her a quelling glance.

A sense of unease traveled up Michelle's spine. Something was going on here. She just wasn't sure what.

Gabe offered his typical warm smile, but there were lines of strain edging his eyes. "How did the delivery go?"

"Figures. It's all about her. *Again*." Finley cast accusing eyes in her dad's direction. "I don't know why I'm even here. No one wants me."

Michelle expected Gabe to crack down on the girl. Unlike Ed, Gabe had never allowed his daughter to speak in such a disrespectful manner.

"Fin, you know that's not true." His tone had a surprisingly gentle quality. His eyes looked more worried than annoyed. "I want you here."

He smiled encouragingly at Michelle, but her throat had closed down. She wasn't sure what he wanted her to do. Or to say.

"Michelle wants you here," he continued in

that same soft and understanding tone when she didn't respond.

"No, really." Finley's eyes flashed blue fire. "She just wants you. I'm someone she has to put up with. If she had her choice, I wouldn't be around."

Michelle's heart stopped.

"Michelle—" Gabe pushed this time "—tell her it's not true."

"It's—" For a second the words stuck in Michelle's throat. "I like you, Finley. You know that. We had fun when you stayed with me. And we had a blast frying the chicken."

"Yeah, we did," Finley grudgingly admitted, gazing down at the ground, her shoulders still stiff.

"Look." Relief filled Gabe's voice. "There's Nick and Lexi."

Finley's head jerked up. For the first time today, Michelle saw her smile.

"Addie." Finley pushed up from her chair and went over to join her friend.

"If you're looking for a place to sit, we have plenty of room right here." Gabe gestured to an open area in front of them.

"Sounds good to me." Nick glanced at Michelle. "If you're sure you don't mind some company?"

"Why would I mind?"

"Well, I've heard things have gotten kind of hot and heavy between you two lately," Nick teased. "I thought you might like some time alone."

"They can't have time alone. I'm in the way," Finley shot back, her tone a mixture of sarcasm and scorn. "Don't you know that?"

"Finley," Gabe spoke sharply.

"Addie and I are going to check out the orchestra up close." Finley lifted her chin as if daring her father to challenge her.

He exhaled a heavy breath. "It's okay with me."

Nick and Lexi exchanged glances.

"Just don't be gone too long," Lexi said to her daughter.

"We won't," the girls said in unison as they hurried away.

"What's up with Finley?" Lexi asked, juggling the fussy toddler in her arms. "She seems upset."

But Lexi didn't get her answer, because at that moment Joel and Kate strolled up with their kids. Soon after, Travis and Mary Karen and their five children arrived to shake things up even more.

For the next hour, Michelle almost forgot about Finley. It was her and Gabe and their friends, just the way she liked it. But when Lexi mentioned she'd like to stretch her legs and asked if anyone wanted to come with her to get a snow cone, Michelle volunteered.

They were approaching the concession stand when Lexi paused and placed a hand on Michelle's arm. "I'm sorry about Nick's remark. I'm sure he's embarrassed, too."

"Where did he get the idea that Gabe and I—"

"—were a couple?" Lexi smiled. "It's kind of obvious. The kiss under the mistletoe. Another hot kiss at the brewery the night of the ground breaking. Everyone is still talking about that one."

"Oh."

"And just so you know, Mrs. McGregor, your neighbor, has had her spyglasses out. She was regaling Nick and anyone else at the courthouse who'd listen about all the kissing you two do in your driveway."

Dear God, it was worse than Michelle thought. She'd thought they'd been subtle, flying under everyone's radar, but they'd fooled no one. Heat crept up her neck.

"I think it's sweet." Lexi squeezed her arm. "I'm happy for you. If you need a caterer for your wedding reception, be sure and keep me in mind."

When flirting with a couple of boys from the youth group hadn't been enough to lift Finley's spirits, she knew even the Blue Hawaiian snow cone Addie had promised to buy her wasn't going to make her feel better.

"My dad and I ran into a woman who's a friend of Shannon." When Finley had heard about the baby, she'd decided she was never going to refer to Shannon as her mother ever again. Shannon didn't want her. Well, that made them even. Finley didn't want Shannon either.

A puzzled frown furrowed Addie's brow. "Shannon, as in your mom?"

"She's not my mother anymore," Finley said. "I used to think she just didn't want to be a mother. Or that she was too young. But she has a baby now and she loves her. It's *me* she doesn't love."

It was as if a giant force was squeezing her insides, bringing an ache to her heart and tears to her eyes, making it difficult to breathe. Finley blinked back the tears and concentrated on her breathing.

Addie's eyes widened. "Your mom, I mean Shannon, has a baby?"

"A girl. Abby. And she really, really loves her." Finley couldn't stop the few tears that leaked from the corners of her lids. "But she can't be bothered to send me a birthday card."

"One day she'll burn in hell." Addie's matter-of-fact tone was at odds with the sympathy in her eyes. "God wouldn't want a monster like her in heaven."

The sentiment provided little solace. All Finley could see was her mo— er, Shannon, hugging and cuddling her new daughter. The daughter she kept. The little girl she loved.

"Did you scream? I like to scream when I'm mad."

Finley exhaled a long breath. "I should have screamed. Instead I took it out on my dad and Michelle. Now they both probably hate me."

The thought brought tears back to Finley's eyes. She was wiping the moisture off on her sleeve when she felt Addie's hand on her arm.

"Don't worry about your dad," Addie said confidently. "He's always stuck by you."

Finley found herself nodding. "My dad once gave up a football scholarship for me."

"That's a humongous deal." Addie sounded suitably impressed. "They don't just give those out to anybody."

"Shannon even tried to get him to give me up so they could go to college and have fun together," Finley confided, recalling a conversation she'd overheard once between her grandparents. "Dad told Shannon he'd never give me up. I was the most important thing in the world to him."

When she'd heard that, Finley's fears had disappeared. She knew then she'd always be able to count on him.

"See?" Addie said. "No worries about him. Now, Michelle…"

"You know, I think she's starting to like me, Addie. Really like me. We had so much fun when I spent the night with her. And yesterday she taught me how to fry chicken."

Addie cocked her head and thought for a moment. "Maybe Michelle could be your mom."

"Maybe." It was the most Finley could say. She was afraid to hope. Scared to tell Addie that when the three of them were together, sometimes she pretended she was out with her mom and dad.

"Look, there's my mom and Michelle." Addie

pointed through the crowd. "They're getting a snow cone, too."

Finley opened her mouth to call out to them, but Addie grabbed her arm. Her eyes twinkled. "Let's sneak up and surprise 'em."

Even though it seemed a little juvenile, the thought of the shock on Lexi's and Michelle's faces made Finley smile. She nodded.

With Addie at her side, the two wove their way through the crowd until they were almost to them. Finley pulled Addie to a stop and put a finger to her lips when she heard her name.

"Finley is a nice girl," Michelle said with a sigh. "But like most teenagers she can be moody and difficult at times."

The smile on Finley's lips faded and a roar filled her ears. Unfortunately the roar wasn't loud enough to drown out all the rest of Michelle's words.

"…marry Gabe."

"You wouldn't marry him because of Finley?" Lexi sounded shocked.

Michelle lowered her voice then, but Finley had already heard enough.

Addie looked at Finley, eyes wide. "I'm sure she didn't mean it."

Finley grabbed her friend's arm and pulled her quickly in the opposite direction. Even once they were far away from the concession stand, Michelle's words still rang in her ears.

"You can't tell anyone what we heard. Understand?"

"I'm sure she didn't mean it," Addie repeated, looking as if she was about to cry.

Finley pressed her lips together. "She meant it."

Now Finley just had to decide what she was going to do about it.

"Something is wrong with Finley." Gabe handed Michelle a bowl filled with salad, then picked up a platter of steaks.

The clear evening was a perfect one to grill out. Gabe had even added extra dried cranberries to the salad because they were Finley's favorite.

Michelle had barely seen the girl since the Fourth of July festivities last week. Later that night, Gabe had told her about running into a friend of Finley's mother. Just hearing Gabe recount the story made Michelle angry. She understood why the girl had been so belligerent.

The knowledge made Michelle feel even worse about voicing those old doubts to Lexi. Thank goodness she'd also made it clear to her friend that she'd changed her mind.

"She's been different." Gabe opened the French door leading to the deck and motioned her outside. "There's this look of profound sadness in her eyes that I've never seen before."

"Have you spoken with her?"

"That's the crazy thing." Gabe placed the steaks on the grill. "She won't talk to me. We've always been able to talk with each other."

His phone buzzed just as Michelle opened her mouth.

"Do you mind if I take this? It's my mom. My

dad has been having some medical tests. So far so good. But—"

Michelle waved him silent. "Answer it."

She pointed to the doorway, offering him privacy, but he shook his head.

"Hi, Mom. Everything okay with Dad?" His expression stilled. "No, Finley isn't here right now. I'm expecting her any moment."

As he listened, Michelle saw a range of emotions cross his face. "This has to be some kind of mistake. She'd never…yes, I will speak with her. I'll call you later."

"What's going on?" Michelle asked. "Is something wrong?"

"It's Finley," he stammered. "She called my parents and told them she hates it here and wants to live with them."

## *Chapter Nineteen*

Years ago, Gabe had gotten walloped in the chest with a two-by-four. All the air had been forced from his lungs and he'd lain on the ground struggling to breathe. He remembered that feeling. He felt that way now.

"She wants to live with your parents?" Michelle pulled her brows together. "In Florida?"

The startled look on her face didn't surprise him. Michelle knew Finley was close to her grandparents. There were pictures of them scattered throughout the house and Finley talked fondly of them.

But why would his daughter want to leave him? It didn't make sense.

A door slammed in the other part of the house.

"She's home," Michelle murmured. "It's best I leave."

"No." Gabe took her hand. "Stay. I'm sure this is simply a misunderstanding. My mother has been under so much pressure because of my dad going through all these tests that she probably misunderstood."

Seconds later, Finley appeared in the doorway. Her gaze slid from Michelle to him to the grill. "I'm not hungry."

"Not so fast," Gabe said when she turned to leave. "I need to talk to you about something."

The suddenly bored expression told him nothing.

"Grandma called. She said you want to live with them?"

He waited for his daughter to laugh, to say she'd

just asked to *visit* them. After all, their home was in a fifty-five plus retirement community. Why would she ever want to live there?

Finley gave a curt nod. "That's right."

Gabe felt an icy fist of fear clench his heart. "But why? I thought you were happy in Jackson."

"Well, you thought wrong." Finley said in a matter-of-fact tone. "I haven't been happy since we moved here. I've just been pretending. But I'm tired of pretending."

Could it be true? Had he totally misread the situation? "Surely I'd have noticed if you were that unhappy—"

"You've been too busy to notice," Finley sneered, her words sharp as a knife and designed to wound. "It's always been that way. You work all these hours. Then when you are finally home, you want to spend time with your—" her gaze shifted to Michelle and her upper lip curled "—friends."

Gabe's heart stuttered. "Finley, you have to know how much you mean to me."

"You've done your duty." Her lips pressed together. "With me gone you'll be free to live your life without a kid always in the way."

He reached out to her, but she took a step back and shook her head.

"If I ever made you feel that you were an imposition, I'm sorry." Even though his daughter hadn't moved an inch from her position in the doorway, Gabe could feel her slipping further away with each passing second. "That's not how I feel. I don't want you to go. Please—"

"I don't want to live here with you anymore." Finley lifted her chin. "You need to accept that and move on. Forget I even exist."

Gabe crossed the distance between them in several long strides and pulled his daughter close. "I love you, Finley girl. I have from the moment I first saw you. Whatever is wrong, we can work it out. I promise."

For a second, he swore she hugged him back. But just as hope surged, she jerked from his arms and shot him a look of disdain. "I'm going to live with Grandma and Grandpa. If you try to stop me, I'll run away. Then you'll never see me again."

"Finley, honey, I don't understand—"

"Trust me." She met his gaze. "It won't just be better for me, it'll be better for you, too."

Finley was scheduled to fly to Florida on Saturday. Gabe had tried everything to convince her to stay, but she wouldn't budge. If he wouldn't let her go to Florida, she'd run away.

Gabe had told Michelle his parents were confident that after a week in their retirement community, she'd beg to return to Jackson Hole. Gabe wasn't so sure.

Michelle couldn't shake the feeling that Finley's actions had something to do with her. But how could that be? She'd spent the last three days trying to think why Finley was doing this when she so clearly loved her father, but kept coming up blank.

Her last appointment of the day had cancelled

and instead of heading over to the hospital, she'd come to Hill of Beans hoping a caramel macchiato pick-me-up would be just what the doctor ordered. So far, it hadn't improved her mood, but then she'd only gotten to the whipped cream.

"Your office manager thought I'd find you here." Looking bright and sunny in a yellow linen suit, Lexi dropped into the chair on the opposite side of the table.

"How's Addie holding up?" Michelle knew that Lexi's daughter had been inconsolable when she'd heard the news.

"She and I had a long talk this morning." Lexi's amber eyes met Michelle's. "I think I discovered why Finley's leaving."

"Did you tell Gabe?" Michelle straightened in her seat. "If he knows why, he may be able to convince her to stay."

Lexi cocked her head. "Are you sure that's what you want?"

Michelle wasn't sure what kind of game Lexi was playing but it had to stop. Gabe's future happiness was at stake. "Of course that's what I want. Gabe has been miserable."

"But if Finley is gone, then you and Gabe can be together." Lexi's eyes never left Michelle's face. "No teenage daughter in the home. Isn't that what you said you wanted?"

"I said that's how I *used* to feel. But I also made it clear my feelings had changed." In fact, hearing those words flow from her lips had made Michelle realize how wrong she'd been to ever think that way. She'd come to a simplistic conclusion to a complex issue. She'd made herself believe that Ed's daughters were the root of her marital problems, taking the onus off her and Ed.

"Well, that's not what Finley thinks."

A sinking feeling filled the pit of Michelle's stomach. "What are you saying?"

"She overheard us talking by the concession stand. But only bits and pieces. She drew her own conclusion." A pained look crossed Lexi's face. "Addie thinks Finley is leaving to pave the way for you and Gabe to be together. She wants her father to be happy."

Michelle brought her fingers to her lips. "Oh, my God. Is that what this is all about?"

As Lexi slowly nodded, the puzzle pieces clicked into place. Suddenly it all made sense.

Gabe had been hurt. Finley had been hurt.

*Because of me.*

Michelle buried her face in her hands. Finley was willing to sacrifice her own happiness for her father. Her admiration for the teenager inched up another notch. She was a child any man or woman could be proud to call their daughter... including her.

"Michelle." Lexi's hand squeezed her shoulder. "You have to stop her from leaving."

Michelle lifted her head and drew in a deep breath. "Trust me, I'll take care of everything."


"Thank you both for giving me this time." Michelle took a seat in a chair, her palms sweaty, her heart pounding in her chest. "There's a lot I have to say."

Finley and Gabe sat at opposite ends of the sofa directly across from her. The girl had been griping when Michelle arrived about needing the time to finish packing for her early morning flight, but Gabe had insisted she could give Michelle fifteen minutes of her time.

"Go ahead." Gabe offered an encouraging smile. There were dark circles under his eyes and he looked as if he hadn't slept in days. "We're listening."

Finley's gaze was directed out the French doors.

"If there was a lesson to be learned from the failure of my first marriage, it was the importance of communication."

Even though Gabe had already heard the story, Finley hadn't, so Michelle went on to talk about what had gone on with her stepdaughters and her first husband.

"That's all very interesting." Gabe looked puzzled. "But I'm not sure of the point."

"The point is twofold." Michelle took a breath. "The first is the failure of that marriage rested in the lack of communication between Ed and me. I initially blamed his daughters when the fault was with the two adults in the house."

This next part wasn't going to be quite as easy.

"After the breakup of my marriage, I vowed that I'd never be with a man who had teenagers—especially daughters—in the home."

"You'd decided you didn't want a teenage stepdaughter?" Gabe's brows slammed together. "Then what the hell were you doing seeing me?"

"I didn't plan for things to get serious." She glanced at Finley. "And you misunderstood what I said to Lexi."

Gabe gave her a long, hard stare. "What did you say?"

"I told Lexi that I'd initially been convinced that you weren't the man for me."

"Because of Finley." The tiny muscle in his jaw jumped.

"Initially," Michelle admitted, hating the hurt

she saw mixed with the anger in his eyes. "But then I got to know and care for Finley. And I came to realize how wrong I was to blame Ann and Chrissy. Ed and I deserved the blame. We were the adults."

Michelle turned to Finley, who looked stunned. "You heard only part of the conversation. I was angry with you, yes, over how you were acting. But you missed the part when I told Lexi how much you'd come to mean to me."

"What does all this have to do with Finley leaving?" Gabe was pale beneath his tan.

"Finley thought I told Lexi I'd never marry a man with a teenager." Michelle found a certain relief in getting it all out in the open. "I believe Finley is leaving because she wants you to be happy. She thinks I won't marry you as long as she is here."

Michelle took a deep breath and included Finley in her gaze. "I am so sorry."

The disappointment on Gabe's face tore at her heartstrings. The anger in his eyes was no more than she deserved. Gabe and Finley had suffered because of her mistakes. She'd almost broken up his family. If he decided to never speak to her again, Michelle knew she deserved that, too.

"I am so angry with you right now." There was a chill to his voice she'd never heard before. "If you had issues with Finley's behavior, you should have said so to her, to *us,* not shared it with Lexi."

Michelle hung her head. She opened her mouth to agree but Finley spoke first.

"Daddy—" Finley stood and moved to his side "—it's not just Michelle who needs to apologize. I did some pretty rotten things myself."

"You were upset about your mother that day," he said. "That I can understand."

His gaze remained focused on Michelle, the look in his eyes telling her it was *her* behavior that had hurt him.

"Not just that day, Daddy." Finley clasped her hands together and visibly swallowed. "Even before then I—I could see you and Michelle were getting close. I got worried. I wanted to make sure she was the right one for you."

Twin lines of confusion notched between Gabe's brows. "I don't understand."

Michelle didn't either, but she remained silent, letting the girl speak.

"I did a couple of tests."

Finley spoke so softly that Michelle wasn't sure she'd heard correctly.

"Tests?" Gabe's right eyebrow lifted. "What kind of tests?"

As if worried she wasn't going to have time to get everything out, with rapid-fire speed, Finley began to explain.

When she told her dad how she'd deliberately left him home when he was sick to see if Michelle would take care of him, the confusion on Gabe's face deepened.

"But Michelle is a doctor." Gabe looked perplexed. "Of course she'd take care of someone who was sick."

"She takes care of ladies having babies," Finley reminded him. "You're a man."

"Good point." Michelle felt a stab of hope when she saw Gabe's lips twitch. Finley had been through a lot. However this ended up for her and Gabe, Michelle didn't want the good relationship he'd enjoyed with his daughter damaged.

"Michelle took good care of me." The hard look in Gabe's eyes softened.

"She passed that test," Finley agreed. "But that wasn't the worst thing I did."

Instead of interrupting, Gabe simply waited. Michelle did the same.

"Before that…" Finley clasped her now-trembling hands together in front of her. "I had Sasha…kidnapped."

"You did what?" Gabe roared.

Finley jumped back.

"I wanted to see how Michelle would react under stress." The words tumbled from Finley's mouth, one after the other. "I know how much she loves Sasha and I—"

"You put that dog in harm's way for a test?" Gabe's eyes flashed golden fire and his voice grew louder with each word.

"Sasha was always safe." Finley quickly reassured her father before turning beseeching eyes on Michelle. "You have to believe me. I love Sasha. I'd never let anything bad happen to her."

There were a thousand things Michelle could have pointed out to her at that moment, but then she'd made her share of mistakes, too.

She offered Finley a reassuring smile. "I know you care about Sasha and would never do anything to harm her."

Gratitude mingled with relief in Finley's eyes. But if she thought her father would be as understanding and give her a pass on this one, she was mistaken.

"I don't know where you took Sasha or how all the events of that evening fell together, but I do know that things could have gone wrong despite whatever safeguards you'd put in place." He looked flushed and annoyed but spoke in a quiet, controlled tone. "A person's life and emotions, an animal's life, is nothing to tinker with and manipulate."

"I know that now." Finley looked properly chastised. "And I'm sorry."

"It's not just me you owe an apology." He shifted his gaze to Michelle.

"I'm sorry, Michelle." Tears welled up and spilled over in the girl's eyes.

Michelle was instantly at Finley's side, gathering the girl in her arms. "I forgive you," she whispered against the soft brown hair. "And I'm sorry, too, so very sorry. It wasn't you. I was just scared of being in the same situation again."

Finley tightened her hold. "I forgive you."

A feeling of peace stole over Michelle. For a second she believed everything would be okay. Until she saw Gabe's face.

## Chapter Twenty

"I'll call Grandma and tell her I'm not coming." Finley released her hold on Michelle. She started out of the room but Gabe called her back.

He stared for a moment, studying her intently. "Promise me you'll never run from a difficult situation again."

"I won't." Finley lifted her chin. "I'm a Davis. I forgot that for a while. I won't forget it again."

"And I want you to talk to Dr. Allman about the issues with your mother," Gabe said firmly.

For a second Finley looked like she was going to argue then she nodded. "I will."

"Okay." A smile touched his mouth. "Tell Grandma and Grandpa I'll call them later."

Finley was almost to the door when she stopped. "Can Addie spend the night this weekend?"

"Not when you're grounded."

There was a long silence. Finley shifted from one foot to the other. "Ah, exactly how long am I grounded?"

"Two weeks."

Relief crossed her face. "Good. I thought it'd be more."

Gabe opened his mouth to respond, but Finley continued before he could speak. "And, Dad, if you want to marry Michelle, I'm all for it. As long as I get to be a bridesmaid."

The stunned look on Gabe's face was almost comical as he watched Finley dance from the room.

Michelle only wished her heavy heart could be so light. Right now it was shrouded in darkness.

A darkness she'd brought on herself. She moistened her lips. She had to clear her throat before she could speak.

"I'm sorry, Gabe. I never meant to hurt you or Finley. I love you. And I love her, too." Her eyes flooded and she wiped them with her palm. "What a time to finally say it, huh? Just when everything between us is imploding."

Her attempt at a laugh sounded more like a sob.

His gaze searched her face. He gestured to the sofa. "I'd like to talk."

With her heart hammering in her chest, Michelle took a seat on one end. He dropped down beside her.

"It appears for you marrying a man with kids was the ultimate deal breaker?"

"Yes, well," she said, conscious of the fact that while he sat less than a foot away, there had never been a greater distance between them. "I'd always believed that marriage was for life. Then I married Ed and, no matter how much I tried, I couldn't make it work. It was him and his daughters on one side and me on the other. I couldn't take the chance of that happening again. But—"

There was a long speculative pause when she didn't continue. "But?" he prompted.

"I now see that the dysfunction in those family dynamics had more to do with Ed and me than with the girls." She clenched her fingers together in her lap. "If we could have communicated better, worked as a team…"

While she was talking he'd moved closer.

"The experience didn't sour you on all men." Gabe twirled a strand of hair between his fingers.

She expelled a shaky breath, realizing he was actually touching her again. "No."

By now he was so close that Michelle could see the grains of dark stubble on his cheek and the smooth firmness of his lips. She remembered how he tasted and felt a sharp, sweet stab in her heart. If only she could turn back time…

"When Shannon and I were together, she'd talk to her girlfriends about her concerns and fears, not to me." His gaze searched hers. "She was young. I understand that now. But I firmly believe for a relationship to be strong, each partner has to be willing to be honest and share their feelings with each other."

"You're right." Michelle expelled a shaky breath. "I didn't do that with you. But I've learned my lesson...."

A lesson she would carry with her the rest of her life. A life she might very well have to live without Gabe. Or Finley.

How could she have been so blind? Happiness, love, a family of her own had been so close. Right next door.

Michelle's heart shifted painfully in her chest.

"I wish I could take away the pain of your failed marriage," she heard him murmur. "But I can't. I can only show you that that isn't how it has to be."

Michelle pulled her thoughts back to the present. What was he saying?

"You said your experience didn't sour you on

men." Gabe raked a hand through his hair. "How about on marriage?"

An electricity filled the air, jolting Michelle back to life.

"I'd be willing to consider an offer of marriage from the right man." Michelle was surprised by how rational and calm she sounded when her insides were quaking. "Under the right circumstances."

"Say you had found the right man." Gabe paused, clearing his throat roughly. "What would be the right circumstances?"

"Well, it would have to be a surprise, because I love surprises," she said breathlessly, her heart beating salsa rhythm against her ribs. "And he'd have to get down on one knee."

"What about a ring?"

Her gaze locked with his.

"Not absolutely necessary if the proposal was spontaneous," Michelle whispered, even though they were the only two in the room.

"Any other circumstances I, er, he'd need to know?"

Mesmerized, Michelle stared into those beautiful amber eyes and shook her head slowly. "All that would matter is that he loved me as much as I love him."

Gabe slipped from the sofa and dropped to his knee. When he took her hand, Michelle gasped. "Now? Here?"

"I can't think of a better place or time." Gabe gazed into her eyes. "I love you, Michelle Kerns. I can't imagine my life without you in it."

"I can't imagine my life without you either," she managed to choke out.

"Will you make me the happiest man in the world by agreeing to be a wife to me and a mother to Finley and any other children we might have?"

"Yes, yes. Oh, yes." Tears of joy slipped down her cheeks and suddenly she was in his arms and his lips were on hers.

When they came up for air, she laid her head

against his chest and listened to the reassuring, steady beat of his heart.

"You know," she said, toying with a button on his shirt, "I wouldn't mind if Finley came with us on our honeymoon."

Gabe had already started shaking his head before Michelle finished talking. "I'd do anything for you, sweetheart, but that's not happening. Finley can stay with Addie or her grandparents while we're gone. The honeymoon is our time together. They'll be plenty of opportunities for family vacations later."

"Family." She rolled the word around her tongue, liking the feel of it.

As his lips lowered to hers once again, Michelle realized she'd received a true double blessing.

Not only Mr. Right, but a wonderful daughter, as well. And hopefully many more children to fill their home with laughter and love.

# *Epilogue*

Michelle stood in the foyer of the small church on a beautiful fall day in Jackson Hole, butterflies in her stomach. Her lace wedding dress with the V-shaped neckline and cap sleeves had been the one her mother had worn almost forty years earlier.

Her bridesmaids, Lexi and Adrianna, had stepped back to give her some time alone with her maid of honor, her soon-to-be daughter, Finley. The girl looked surprisingly grown up in her eggplant A-line satin dress.

Impulsively Michelle reached forward to clasp Finley's hands in hers. She met her gaze. "Today I'll promise to your father to love, honor and cherish him all the days of my life. I want you to know I'll mean every word."

A slight smile lifted Finley's lips. "I know you love him."

"And I also vow to love, honor and cherish you as my daughter all the days of my life." Michelle hurriedly blinked back tears as the emotion in her heart welled up and threatened to spill over. "You may not have been born to me, Finley, but I couldn't love you more. I can't imagine my life without you in it."

"I love you, too…" Finley's voice shook. "Because you're marrying my dad, is it okay if I call you Mom?"

The hopeful look in the girl's eyes tugged at Michelle's heartstrings.

"I'd be honored," Michelle whispered, the words thick with emotion.

"I hate to break this up." Michelle's father interrupted, holding out his arm. "But your groom awaits."

Michelle realized that Lexi and Adrianna had already started down the aisle. Before she took her dad's arm, she gave Finley a heartfelt hug.

"Gabe is a good man." Her father's voice was low and gravelly as he maneuvered them to the end of the aisle. "You two are going to be very happy. And your mom and I are thrilled we're not only getting a fabulous son-in-law but also a wonderful granddaughter."

After Finley started down the blue carpet, Michelle and her dad moved into position. It was then that she saw Gabe, resplendent in a black tux, waiting for her at the front of the church.

The look in his eyes dispelled the last of her nervousness. It was all there. The love, the caring, the until-death-do-us-part.

"Ready, honey?" her father whispered.

She nodded, eager to start her new life with the man she loved.

\* \* \* \* \*